A PASSIONATE AFFAIR

D0588225

'Jay Ravek is not in your league,'
someone had told Cassandra—and what
with that, and her reluctance to get
involved with any more men anyway,
after her unhappy experience of marriage, that would seem to be that. But
it wasn't!

A PASSIONATE AFFAIR

BY

ANNE MATHER

MILLS & BOON LIMITED
15–16 BROOK'S MEWS
LONDON W1A 1DR

First published 1982
Australian copyright 1982
Philippine copyright 1982
This edition 1982

© Anne Mather 1982

ISBN 0 263 74031 5

Set in Monophoto Times 10 on 11 pt.
01–1282 – 54077

Made and printed in Great Britain by
Richard Clay (The Chaucer Press) Ltd,
Bungay, Suffolk

CHAPTER ONE

'Who did you say that man was?'

Cassandra tried not to give her words emphasis, but Liz was too highly attuned to the inflections in her tone to be deceived for long.

'What man?' she asked, turning a rather bemused face from her contemplation of the large square canvas in front of her, and Cassandra signalled with her eyes, the object of her enquiry evident. 'Oh—you mean Jay Ravek!' Liz's mouth assumed a sardonic twist. 'Darling, don't think of it. Don't even consider it. He's far too uncivilised for you.'

'Uncivilised?' Discretion gave way to mild incredulity, as Cassandra allowed her gaze to rest briefly on the tall dark man presently in conversation with Damon Stafford, near the entrance to the gallery. She shrugged. 'He looks highly civilised to me.'

'Don't they always?' Liz adopted a thoughtful pose. 'I mean,' she went on, 'who would think, looking at a tiger, looking at its lean symmetry, at its grace and beauty, that it was the most unscrupulous predator ever created?'

Cassandra sighed. 'All right, Liz, you've made your point—about tigers, anyway. But just because you may be strongly into cats at the moment, that has no bearing on my question about Jay Ravek.'

'Oh, but it does.' Liz's long-nailed fingers curved about her arm. 'Cass, my love, I know what you've said, and believe me, I can guess how you feel. But getting involved with a man like Jay Ravek——'

'Who said anything about getting involved?' Cassandra's brows arched impatiently. 'Liz, you must stop treating me like a china doll! I'm not. I never have been. If I were, Mike would have broken me long ago.'

Liz studied her friend's face with genuine concern. 'But you're not denying that Mike has left you with a— how shall I say it?—a chip on your shoulder, hasn't he?' She paused. 'Not all men are like Mike, Cass. Remember that.'

'I do remember it.' Cassandra felt vaguely indignant that Liz should feel it necessary to speak to her in this way. 'Look—if I'd let Mike poison my mind, I wouldn't be interested in any other man, would I?'

'No.' Liz conceded that point. 'But I just don't want you to get hurt again, that's all. And—well, Jay Ravek has quite a reputation for hurting people, women particularly.'

Cassandra expelled her breath quickly. 'Liz, I only asked who the man was. I didn't say I was going to climb into bed with him!'

Liz bowed her head. 'All right, all right, I'm sorry!' Her hand fell to her side. 'But pick someone else to re-sharpen your claws on. Jay Ravek is not in your league.'

Cassandra wanted to protest that she was not the innocent Liz thought she was, but she doubted her friend would believe her. All Liz knew was that she had had one bad marriage, and the deeper implications of that statement had never been discussed between them. Liz had been too discreet to ask and Cassandra had felt too raw to tell her immediately after Mike's death, and now, nine months later, the subject was too difficult to broach.

'So——' Liz changed the subject. 'What do you think of Stafford's work? I must admit I don't really under-stand it, but he's had such wonderful reviews it must be good.'

'Not necessarily.' Cassandra was still brooding over their earlier conversation. 'Just because it's received cri-

tical acclaim, it doesn't mean it's unequivocally good.'
She grimaced. 'I think it's ghastly, quite honestly. All
those heads appearing from nowhere—it's positively
gruesome!'

'That's what I like, an honest opinion.'

The two girls started with equal degrees of dis-
concertment, but Cassandra's confusion was compounded of embarrassment and a certain amount of
apprehension. Damon Stafford was standing right
behind them, his arms folded across his chest, his
bearded face alight with amusement, and right beside
him stood Jay Ravek.

'Oh—Damon!' Liz recovered her composure with
immaculate ease, her wide mouth spreading in an
apologetic smile. 'You know what they say about
eavesdroppers, don't you, darling? And Cass was only
being bitchy, weren't you, love?'

Cassandra's fingers clutched her bag more tightly.
'I'm afraid I know nothing about modern art, Mr
Stafford,' she offered, intensely conscious of Jay Ravek's
dark eyes upon her. 'You must forgive me if you think I
was rude. Naturally my opinion is of no importance.'

'On the contrary, Miss—er——'

'*Mrs*,' Cassandra corrected him formally. 'Roland.'

'Well, Mrs Roland,' Damon Stafford smiled, 'anyone
will tell you, I'm always interested in the opinion of a
beautiful woman.'

Cassandra blushed, she couldn't help it, and Liz
uttered a relieved laugh. 'Very nicely put, Damon,' she
complimented him drily. 'You really shouldn't put
people on the spot like that. It's not nice.'

'Oh, I'm sure Mrs Roland will forgive me.' Damon
glanced sideways at the man beside him, as if for confirmation, and then, turning back to Cassandra, he
said: 'Let me offer you some more champagne, Mrs
Roland. Your glass appears to be empty.'

'Thank you, but no.' Cassandra covered the rim of

her glass with her palm as Damon turned to summon one of the white-coated attendants circulating among the guests at the reception. 'We—er—we were just leaving, weren't we, Liz? I for one have to get back to work.'

'What is your work, Mrs Roland?'

It was Jay Ravek who had spoken, and Cassandra's tongue appeared, to moisten her upper lip as she was obliged to answer his question. 'I'm an interior designer, Mr Ravek.'

It was not until after she had finished speaking that she realised she had used his name without thinking. The faint quirk of his mouth might have indicated his observance of that fact, but if he had been about to make a comment, Liz forestalled her.

'And she's very good at it, too,' she declared, giving Cassandra a knowing smile that the other girl found quite annoying. 'She only started the business six months ago, and already she's gaining quite a reputation.'

'Really?' Damon sounded impressed, but Cassandra wanted to die of embarrassment.

'It's a very small business really,' she insisted, giving Liz a quelling look, but her friend just arched her brows at her and was obviously unrepentant.

'Perhaps I could contact you about my apartment,' remarked Damon, pulling a notebook out of his pocket. 'What did you say the name was? Roland? I'll make a note of that.'

'It's Ro-Allen, actually,' Liz inserted, looking over his shoulder. 'Ro-Allen Interiors. Chris Allen is Cass's partner. He has a brilliant eye for colour.'

'Liz!'

Cassandra was furious, but Liz only shrugged her shoulders. 'Contacts, darling—that's what it's all about. Don't you agree, Mr Ravek? In your work, you must find I'm right.'

'If you say so, Miss Lester.' Jay Ravek's lean face was sardonic. 'However, we don't all have your opportunities for contacting the right people.'

Liz's rather pointed features seemed to sharpen, but she bit her tongue on what she would obviously have liked to retort, and took Cassandra's arm. 'Time to go, darling,' she declared pleasantly. 'We mustn't outstay our welcome.'

'You couldn't do that,' Damon replied gallantly. 'I'll look forward to reading your comments. Oh——' he glanced at the man beside him again, '——and don't be too hard on Jay, will you? You columnists have given him a pretty raw deal, one way and another.'

'Perhaps it's nothing more than he deserves,' observed Liz with a tight smile. 'Goodbye, Damon. Thanks for the champagne. It was delightful!'

The Seely Gallery occupied the upper floor of a building in South Molton Street, and the two girls emerged from the shadowy stairwell into the watery sunshine of a November afternoon. It wasn't particularly cold, but it was damp, and Cassandra thrust her hands into the pockets of her suede coat and hunched her shoulders in a momentary shiver.

'Bastard!' said Liz, with unexpected fervour, and Cassandra gazed at her in surprise.

'Who?' she exclaimed, although she could guess. 'Jay Ravek? Why? What did he say to upset you?'

'It isn't what he says, it's what he doesn't say,' declared Liz venomously. 'Arrogant swine! Making insinuations about my friends, about my family——'

'Did he do that?' Cassandra shook her head. 'You really don't like him, do you?' She paused. 'What does he do anyway?'

Liz stared at her disbelievingly. 'You must have heard of him!'

'No, I haven't.'

'But I assumed you'd recognised his name.' Liz

sighed. 'He's quite famous—or notorious, whatever way you look at it. He writes for the *Post*. He's one of their correspondents, generally overseas—when he's not in London, making it with every rich bird in town!'

Cassandra's wide forehead furrowed. 'Oh—yes, I seem to remember reading something about him.'

'You would,' agreed Liz grimly. 'I told you, he's bad news. So don't go getting any ideas about him, because believe me, you'd regret it.'

Cassandra felt a recurring twinge of resentment. 'Liz, I am over twenty-one. And I was married for five years. I know how to look after myself.'

'Mike Roland was a choirboy compared to Jay Ravek,' Liz retorted, turning up the collar of her fur jacket. 'Take my word for it, kid. You don't need another bad experience.'

Walking back to the studio in a mews off Great Portland Street, Cassandra had plenty of time to mull over the things Liz had said. She meant well, Cassandra supposed, but the ten years' seniority Liz possessed always gave her the edge. They had known one another for more than seven years. They had met at an exhibition just like this one. But Cassandra couldn't help wishing Liz would not always treat her as if she was incapable of handling her own life. She had made mistakes, of course, and her disastrous marriage to Mike Roland was still uppermost in her mind. But Mike was dead now, after all the heartache it had caused her, that period of her life was over and she badly wanted to forget it. Liz's frequent references to her marriage prevented her from doing so, continually reminding her of her declared determination not to be fooled again. What Liz didn't appear to understand was that just because she had had a bad time with Mike, and had no desire to repeat the experience, it did not mean she could not find the opposite sex attractive. She did. Or at least, some members of it. And Jay Ravek was certainly a very attractive member . . .

She found Chris Allen hunched over his drawing board when she entered the offices of Ro-Allen Interiors some fifteen minutes later. The air was thick with to-bacco smoke and the inevitable cigarette drooped from the corner of his mouth. Cassandra breathed a sigh of protest and marched to the windows, flinging them wide despite the chilling afternoon air, and her partner turned to her resignedly, pressing the stub of the cigarette out in the dish already overflowing beside him.

'You'll kill yourself with those filthy things!' ex-claimed Cassandra, taking off her coat and hanging it on one of a row of hooks screwed to the wall behind her desk.

'It's my life,' observed Chris laconically, sliding off his stool. 'We can't all be invited to champagne recep-tions, hobnobbing with the *crème de la crème*! Besides,' he fumbled in his pocket for his pack of cigarettes, placing a fresh one between his lips, 'they help me to concentrate, and right now, I need some inspiration.'

Cassandra, seated at her desk, looked up at the young man before her with grudging affection. She knew how hard he was working to make the business a success, and Liz had not been joking when she said he had a brilliant eye for colour. If Cassandra's abilities lay in looking at a room and being able to judge its potentialities, Chris's talent was for colouring her work, giving it life and beauty. His was the skill that combined furniture with fabric, and substantiated her spartan drawings with light and detail. At twenty-five, he was precisely ten months older than she was, and their asso-ciation came from way back, when Cassandra, like him, was a student at the London School of Textile Design. Those were the days before Mike Roland came into her life, when she had still been uncertain of what she really wanted to do. At least her marriage to Mike had taught her that that kind of one-to-one relationship was not what she wanted, and although she would not have wished him dead, her freedom seemed particularly precious to her now.

'So——' Chris flicked his lighter and applied it to the end of his cigarette. 'Was there anybody interesting at the reception? What did you think of Stafford's work?'

Cassandra chose to answer his second question first. 'Quite frankly, I thought his paintings were horrible,' she admitted candidly. 'I didn't like them, and I certainly didn't understand them.'

'Shades of Hieronymus Bosch,' remarked Chris drily, putting his lighter away, and at her look of incomprehension, he added: 'He was a Dutch painter of the fifteenth or sixteenth century, I'm not sure which. But his work was very pessimistic, and I've heard it said that Stafford's is the same.'

Cassandra's lips twitched. 'You're very well informed.'

'Not really.' Chris made a deprecatory gesture. 'He had a marvellous use of colour, which I admire, and which no one else has successfully been able to imitate. And besides,' he shrugged irrepressively, 'I watched a programme about him on television, a couple of nights ago.'

Cassandra made a face and flung a pencil at him as Chris ducked back to his drawing board. He laughed and resumed his seat, and leaving her own, Cassandra came to look over his shoulder.

'Hey, that's good!' she exclaimed, pulling her spectacles out of their case and sliding them on to her nose so that she could look more closely. She had discovered she was long-sighted only two months before, when after a series of headaches she had sought professional advice. In consequence, she now wore wide hornrims when she was working, and their size gave an added charm to her pale oval features.

Chris glanced sideways at her, his blue eyes alight

with enthusiasm. 'Do you think so?' he asked. 'Do you really think so? You don't think I've gone over the top with all this dark oak and heavy wallpaper?'

'Of course not.' Cassandra straightened, smiling down into his lean good-looking features. 'Chris, they told us what they wanted. They want us to restore the house's original character. They want oak panelling and figured damask. They want velvet curtains and leather-bound books in the library.' She shook her head. 'I don't suppose it really matters what the books are. You could put *The Decameron* up there, and they'd never notice. But,' she grimaced, 'so long as they're happy, and they're prepared to pay for it—who are we to object?'

Chris pulled thoughtfully at his nose, a habit he had when he was worried, and then looked doubtfully up at her. 'Is that really how you feel?' he asked, with sudden gravity, and she turned away and walked back to her desk, as if she needed to consider her response.

'No,' she conceded at last, perching on the edge of her desk and chewing at the earpiece of the spectacles she had removed from her nose. 'But, Chris,' she sighed, 'we can only offer advice. If people refuse to take it . . .'

'I don't like these kind of jobs,' declared Chris flatly. 'I prefer it when we're given a free hand to use the ability that they're paying for!'

'Well, so do I,' exclaimed Cassandra impatiently. 'But we're not in business to create works of art, Chris. And every now and then we have to take a job we don't like.'

Chris hunched his shoulders. 'Well, why the hell did the Steiners employ a firm of interior designers, if they already knew what they wanted? Why didn't they just contract the job out to some painting and decorating company, who'd do a perfectly competent job——'

'Chris, you know why. The Steiners like the idea of——'

'—using our name, I know.'

'Not just that.' Cassandra was honest. 'Any firm of interior designers would do just as well. Only—oh, I suppose they thought we might be more amenable.'

'Because we're just establishing ourselves,' said Chris drily, and Cassandra nodded.

'I guess so. Anyway, Liz said——'

'Liz!' Chris made a sound of derision. 'Just tell Liz from me we'll get our own commissions from now on, will you?'

'Mmm.'

Cassandra's thoughtful response was almost inaudible as she slid off the desk and walked round it to resume her seat. Chris's indignation had struck a slightly distasteful chord in her memory, and she would have preferred not to remember Liz's canvassing of her talents that afternoon. As well as rekindling her embarrassment, it brought Jay Ravek's face too acutely to mind, and her own reactions to his dark intelligent features. She had found him attractive, but then what woman wouldn't? He was tall, but not too tall; lean, but not skinny; and although he was not strictly handsome he possessed the kind of personal magnetism one could only describe as sex appeal. His eyes were almost black and deep-set, accentuating the heavy lids with their short thick lashes. His nose was straight between high cheek-bones, and his mouth with its thin upper lip and fuller lower one could look both cruel and sensuous.

Cassandra expelled her breath suddenly and pushed her spectacles back on to her nose. He had certainly made an impression, she thought, with a wry grimace. Liz would be horrified if she ever found out just how attractive Cassandra had found him, and her mother-hen qualities would be fully aroused at what she would see as the evidence of Cassandra's vulnerability.

But it wasn't true, Cassandra thought impatiently. Since Mike's death she had met plenty of attractive men, not least Chris himself, who, despite his married state, had made it plain that he still found her as attractive as ever. If she had waited before committing herself to any further emotional entanglements, it was not because she was scared of getting hurt again. On the contrary, she doubted there was a man alive who could hurt her now. Her marriage to Mike had been a disaster, but it had also taught her more about relationships than any other experience could have done. She had entered into that marriage innocently, optimistically, eagerly—and within six months she had been shocked, bruised and disillusioned. Her immature expectations of what a marriage should be had been shattered by the kind of experiences she would have preferred to forget. Mike should never have got married. He liked the company of women far too much; and not just one woman, but many. Later, in her more cynical moments, Cassandra had wondered whether his constant search for satisfaction with women stemmed from his own inability to give satisfaction, and she had been grateful then for his accusations of her frigidity, which meant she was not obliged to suffer his attentions too often. She did not believe she was frigid, however. She had a perfectly normal interest in the opposite sex. If she had never truly enjoyed the act of love, that was not so unusual. She had friends with husbands *and* families who had confessed to a similar deficiency, which, she consoled herself, occurred most frequently with girls of a greater sensitivity. Her experiences were of the mind, rather than the body, she was convinced, and as she enjoyed kissing and caressing and the preliminaries of loveplay, she was unconcerned that so far as Freud was concerned she was unaroused.

It was seven o'clock before she left the office. Chris departed around six, and after he had gone, Cassandra abandoned her ideas for an office complex they had been invited to tender for, and gave herself up to the troublesome study of their accounts. Really, she thought, they would soon have to employ an accountant to keep

the books in order. What with income tax returns and
V.A.T. there seemed an inordinate amount of book-
keeping to be done, and although the business was still
in its embryo stages, someone had to ensure that they
did not overreach themselves. At the moment, they had
a good working relationship with a firm of interior de-
corators, who performed the function of translating hers
and Chris's designs into a tangible reality. But eventually
Cassandra hoped to employ their own painters and
plumbers and carpenters, and accomplish every project
themselves, thus ruling out the necessity to rely on con-
tracted labour.

When she finally put down her pen and switched off
the pocket calculator, Cassandra's head was buzzing
with figures. She supposed that sooner or later she
would get used to owing money that she herself was
owed, but right now it seemed a terrifying deficit, and
she massaged her temples wearily as she got up from
her desk.

The studio-cum-office was situated over a pair of
garages, which had once provided stabling for the horses
of a bygone carriage era. Their entrance was via an iron
staircase that ran up the side of the building, and after
locking the door, Cassandra descended the stairs with a
feeling of intense relief. It had been a long day, and she
was tired, and she looked forward eagerly to putting her
feet up on the couch and enjoying a T.V. dinner.

Her small Alfasud was parked in the mews, and she
crossed the cobbled forecourt quickly and inserted her
key in the lock. Chandler Mews was only dimly lit, and
it had crossed her mind on several occasions that it was
an ideal spot for muggers. But so far she had encountered no one but a stray cat, that even so had given
her a nasty scare.

It was cold inside the car, but the engine fired without
a hiccough, and she drove it smoothly out into Great
Portland Street. At this hour of the evening, the traffic

was not hectic, and she turned right towards Tottenham Court Road, and her flat near Russell Square.

She was lucky to have a flat so near to the office, and she never failed to feel grateful for Mike's insurance, which had afforded her enough money to lease the flat and the studio, and provided the capital necessary to start the business. She had not wanted to take the money in the beginning. She had not felt she deserved it. But Mike's mother had been adamant, and with her encouragement she had learned to appreciate her independence. She sometimes wondered whether Mrs Roland's insistence that the money was hers and that she should take it without obligation stemmed from her own experiences with Mike's father. Certainly, the elder Mr Roland had had little consideration for his wife, spending most of his time at the racetrack or on the golf course, and latterly, after his son's involvement in racing, at the Formula One meetings. Unfortuately, he had died before Mike achieved any real success, and his winning of the French Grand Prix was overshadowed by his father's death.

They were both widowed now, and it was through Mrs Roland that Cassandra had found her flat. Mike's mother lived in an apartment in the same building, and while some of her friends had advised her not to live so closely with her in-laws, Cassandra had had no hesitation about accepting. She had never known her own mother and father. They had died when she was only a child, and she had been brought up by her mother's cousin, a spinster lady with no aspirations to motherhood. Still, *Aunt* Esme, as she had preferred to be called, had done her best to give the girl a good home, and if it had been lacking in affection, it had at least given Cassandra her interest in art and design. Aunt Esme taught history at a girls' school in Richmond, but in her spare time she devoured the art galleries, spending hours at the National Gallery or the Tate, reading avidly about painters and sculptors, their lives and their masterpieces, and the influences that coloured their work. It was during the course of these expeditions that Cassandra began to take notice of colour and texture, began to distinguish between the brush-strokes of a master and the amateurish offerings she produced. She learned that there was more to being an artist than the desire to set down on paper or canvas some face full of character, or a colourful London street scene. Her talent lay not in reproducing fine detail but in creating it, in blending together the imaginative with the functional to effect a design, both pleasing and practical. She was not an artist, she was a designer, using other people's art to good advantage, and without Mike's intervention in her life she might well have become a teacher, like Aunt Esme. As it was, she had given up her studies to marry Mike, and Aunt Esme had died before she achieved her ambition to have a studio of her own.

But Mike's mother had nurtured that ambition. From the beginning she had encouraged Cassandra to think for herself, and since Mike's death they had grown so much closer. It was strange, when there was no blood relationship between them, but Mrs Roland came much closer to being the mother she had never had than did Aunt Esme, and Cassandra had never regretted taking the flat which kept them in such close proximity.

Leaving her car in the basement garage, Cassandra took the lift up to the fourth floor with a sense of weariness out of all proportion to the day she had spent. It had seemed such an exhausting day somehow, and at the back of her mind was the suspicion that Jay Ravek had something to do with it. But that was ridiculous, she thought impatiently. She hardly knew the man. They had only exchanged the briefest of words. And yet she knew a nagging sense of disappointment that she would not be seeing him again. That was what was depressing her. He was the first man since Mike she might seriously consider having an affair with, and Liz had made that practically impossible by her vitriolic attitude. If she had not known better, she would have suspected Liz's behaviour to be that of a jealous female, but that could not be so. Liz was a beautiful woman. She was never short of escorts. And if Jay Ravek was as dissolute as Liz said he was, he would obviously have been unable to resist the temptation.

Her flat was not large, consisting simply of a bedroom, a bathroom, a living-room and a kitchen. But it was the first real home of her own she had had, and Cassandra coveted the independence it proclaimed. It was not opulently furnished, but the choice of colours was hers, and the bright banners of green and orange revealed a character searching for its own identity.

Soft lamplight lit on a velvety orange sofa, splashing the rather austere stereo unit with warmth. Cassandra dropped her bag on to the couch, kicked off her shoes, and removed her coat before padding through to the small but stylish kitchen. She depressed the switch on the stereo unit as she passed, releasing the strains of John Lennon's music into the apartment, and determinedly hummed to herself as she extracted her frozen dinner from the fridge. It would be foolish if she allowed thoughts of Jay Ravek to ruin what was left of the evening, she thought, putting the meal into the microwave oven to defrost before cooking. After all, her abstraction over him should warn her that he could be dangerous to her new-found peace of mind, and perhaps her first affair should be with someone who did not stir her emotions so deeply.

The telephone rang as she was making coffee, and leaving the pot percolating, she went to answer it. It was her mother-in-law, and Cassandra relaxed, perching on the arm of the sofa, and cradling the receiver against her ear.

'You're late, darling.' Mrs Roland's voice was warm

with affection. 'I called about half an hour ago, but you were still not home.'

'I've been doing accounts,' remarked Cassandra drily, and heard her mother-in-law's sigh of understanding. 'We really will have to employ an accountant soon. Even with a calculator, my arithmetic isn't up to all the book-keeping we have to do.'

'How about Paul Ludlum?' suggested Mrs Roland at once. 'His father was Henry's accountant for years, and from what I hear, Paul has an excellent reputation. I could speak to him, if you like. Explain the situation. I'm sure he's just the man you need.'

'It sounds interesting,' agreed Cassandra cautiously. 'And it would take a load off my shoulders.' She paused. 'If we can afford it.'

'Of course you can afford it, Cass.' Mrs Roland was adamant. 'You know how well the business is doing. I have every confidence in you.'

'Well—thanks.' Cassandra felt a glow of warmth inside. 'You know, I'd never have had the nerve to do this without you.'

Mrs Roland chuckled. 'It's nice of you to say so, darling, but I don't believe it. You'd have made it, sooner or later. Give yourself the credit, not me.'

'Well, anyway——' Cassandra let the sentence speak for itself, 'I'm about to pour myself a cup of coffee. Would you like one?'

'Oh, darling, I can't.' Mrs Roland was apologetic. 'I'm just on my way out actually. You know—it's my bridge evening.' And as Cassandra acknowledged this with a rueful exclamation, she went on: 'I only rang to let you know I took a phone call for you earlier.'

'A phone call? For me?' Cassandra felt the first twinges of alarm. 'Who was it? And how did you happen to get the call?'

'It was a Mr—Ravek,' declared her mother-in-law, after a moment's hesitation. 'A client, I suppose. He'd found my telephone number in the book under this address, and I assume he expected it was yours. Do you know him?'

'I've—met him.' Cassandra's sense of apprehension was fast giving way to a state of nervous excitement. 'Did—er—did he say what he wanted?'

'Well, he wanted to speak to you, of course,' replied Mrs Roland at once. 'You sound—strange, Cass. Who is he? A boy-friend?'

'No!' Cassandra's response was vehement. 'I—hardly know him.' She paused. 'Did he mention why he wanted to speak to me?'

'No.' Her mother-in-law considered for a moment. 'He asked if you were available, and I explained that I was the wrong Mrs Roland, and he rang off.'

'Oh, I see.' Cassandra could hardly keep the disappointment out of her voice. Obviously he had discovered that there was a *Mrs* Roland listed as living in the building, and assumed it was her. When her mother-in-law explained his mistake, no doubt he had then presumed that she lived with her husband. And as she had only occupied this flat for a little over six months, her number was not in the book. But why had he rung her anyway? And why not at the office? The possibilities were endless, and none of them gave her any satisfaction right now.

'I told him I'd give you the message,' Mrs Roland was saying now, and Cassandra started: 'What message?'

'That he'd rung, of course,' replied her mother-in-law patiently. 'Cass, is there something wrong? This man's not been bothering you, has he?'

'Heavens, no!' Cassandra's laughter was slightly hysterical. 'As I told you, I hardly know him. Er—Liz introduced us, today, at the Stafford reception. You remember—I told you I was going with her.'

'I see.' Mrs Roland sounded intrigued now. 'So who

is he? The name sounds foreign.'

'Well, I don't think he is.' Cassandra felt a sense of relief at being able to talk about him. 'He's a journalist, so Liz says. For the *Post*.'

'Ravek? Ravek?' Mrs Roland said the name over. 'You know, now I come to think of it, the name does sound vaguely familiar. Ravek!' She said it again. 'Yes, I have it. It's Jay Ravek, isn't it?'

'He's that well known, hmm?' remarked Cassandra cynically, remembering Liz's condemnation, but her mother-in-law gave an impatient exclamation.

'No. No, you misunderstand me. I recall reading something about his mother, when she married Sir Giles Fielding—you know, the M.P. He was a barrister before he became interested in politics, and I believe I was introduced to him once at some dinner Henry and I attended. Anyway,' she uttered an apologetic chuckle, 'I'm digressing. What I really wanted to say was that his mother is Russian, her parents' name was Ravekov, and they were émigrés at the end of the last war.'

Cassandra frowned. 'But—if his father's name is Fielding——'

'It's not.' Mrs Roland sighed. 'That's why I remember it. Her son was born long before she became Lady Fielding.'

'I see.' Cassandra drew her lower lip between her teeth.

'I haven't trodden on any toes, have I, Cass?' Her mother-in-law sounded concerned. 'Darling, you mustn't mind my gossiping. I'm sure he's a very nice man.'

'Liz doesn't think so,' said Cassandra flatly. 'She said he was a bastard, and somehow I don't think she meant what you did.'

Mrs Roland clicked her tongue. 'I should hope not! One can hardly blame him for his parents' behaviour.'

'No.' Cassandra felt irritated suddenly. 'Well, he

probably had a commission he wanted to discuss. If he needs to get in touch with me, he can easily do so at the office.'

'Yes . . .' Mrs Roland was thoughtful. 'If you say so, dear.'

'I do.' Cassandra was eager now to put down the phone. 'Have a nice evening, and I'll probably see you tomorrow.'

'Very well, Cass. Goodnight.'

'Goodnight.'

With the telephone receiver restored to its rest, Cassandra lifted her head and caught a glimpse of her reflection in the mirror above the sideboard. She observed with some impatience that she had a smudge of ink on her chin, the result no doubt of supporting her head with the same hand that held her pen, and she rubbed at it absently as she contemplated what she had just learned. Why was Jay Ravek ringing her? What possible reason could he have? And why did it fill her with a sense of apprehension, when she had thought of him constantly since leaving the reception?

She sighed. It wasn't as if she was a raving beauty or anything. She was reasonably tall and slim, and she had lost that angular thinness she had had while Mike was alive, but she was quite ordinary otherwise. She had naturally ash blonde hair, which was always an advantage, but she wore it short, a common enough style nowadays. She had nice skin, the kind that tanned in spite of her blonde hair, but her features were unremarkably regular, and only her eyes attracted any attention. They were large and green, with curling lashes that she darkened, but Mike used to say even they were deceptive. He said they promised so much, but offered so little, and she had never been able to understand why he had married her in the first place. He had had so many girls chasing him in his role as a racing driver, and during their more bitter arguments he had always thrown this up at her.

But that still didn't explain why Jay Ravek wanted to speak to her. It was flattering, of course, and she would not have been human if she had not been curious, but her common sense told her that it might be simpler not to get involved, and perhaps her mother-in-law taking the call was just a blessing in disguise.

CHAPTER TWO

WITH the help of a capsule, Cassandra slept reasonably well, and awakened next morning feeling only mildly lethargic. It was months since she had felt the need for any assistance to sleep, and she had almost forgotten the heady feeling that lingered and the horrible taste in her mouth.

Needing to dispel that sense of inertia, she took a bath before breakfast, and then read the daily paper over her coffee. She was determined not to let thoughts of Jay Ravek disrupt her day as they had disrupted her night, but the latest wave of industrial troubles held little attraction.

Yet the night before she had spent far too much time wondering what his reasons for ringing her had been. After her moments of introspection, she had trudged back into the kitchen, and switched off the percolator without even pouring herself a cup of coffee. She had remained bemused, both by the evidence of the phone call and by what her mother-in-law had told her, and that was why she had taken one of the sleeping capsules the doctor had prescribed for her just after Mike had met his fatal accident. She had needed to sleep, to be alert to face the day—and it was annoying to discover that with consciousness came awareness, and the troubled conviction that Jay Ravek was not going to be that easy to dismiss.

She had an appointment that morning with the manager of a textile warehouse, and when she left the flat soon after nine o'clock, she drove straight to the address in north London. She usually chose the cloth the contractors were to use herself, and she always felt a thrill of excitement as she walked along the rows of bales, fingering their fine texture and admiring the variety of colours. There were so many shades, and such intriguing names for the different colours – oyster satin, damask in a delicious shade of avocado, cream brocade and bronze velvet. There were patterned cottons and rich cretonne, chintz and tufted fabrics, and lengths of chiffon and soft wild silk. Cassandra gained a great deal of satisfaction from choosing the materials, her decision was important, and the exhilaration she obtained more than made up for the long hours of hard work spent at her drawing board.

She and Gil Benedict spent over an hour discussing her requirements and the availability of the order, then she got back into the Alfasud and drove to Chandler Mews.

'Any calls?' she asked casually of Chris, as she shed the jacket of her fringed suede suit, and he lifted his head from the supporting prop of his knuckles and regarded her consideringly.

'One or two,' he conceded, reaching for the inevitable packet of cigarettes, and Cassandra's nerves tightened. 'Holbrook rang to say he can't get those rails for the radiators until next week, and there's been a tentative enquiry from a Mrs Vance, who's apparently seen the Maxwells' flat and would like to discuss us doing something similar for her.'

'Oh.' Cassandra hid her unwelcome sense of disappointment. 'Is that all?'

'Who were you expecting?' Chris was laconic. 'Oh, yes, a man did phone.' He paused as Cassandra's heart accelerated. 'He said his name was—Ludlum, is that right? Something to do with your mother-in-law, I think.'

'Paul Ludlum, yes.' Cassandra's voice was breathy as she sought escape from her foolish thoughts. She crossed the room, and picking up the electric kettle, weighed its contents before plugging it in. 'He's an accountant friend of hers, or rather his father was. She thinks we should have some professional help in that direction.'

'I agree.' Chris lit his cigarette and lay back wearily in his chair. 'God, I'm bushed! Rocky cried on and off all night, and June said it was my turn to keep him quiet.'

Pushing aside her problems, Cassandra managed to smile. 'Don't call him Rocky!' she exclaimed. 'His name's Peter. You know June hates you to make fun of him.'

Chris grimaced. 'He still looks like a horror to me,' he remarked, drawing the nicotine gratefully into his lungs, and Cassandra shook her head as she turned to spoon instant coffee into the cups.

Chris and June had only been married a little over a year, and baby Peter, the main reason for their nuptials, Chris maintained, was now almost six months old. It was typical of Chris that he should choose a nickname for his son, derived from the Rocky Horror Show, but Cassandra was very much afraid that June found this no less unacceptable than Chris's previous decision to give up his well-paid job in the art department of a London television studios to go into partnership with her. Cassandra knew she could never have approached him. She would never have dreamed of asking him to give up so much on the strength of so little. But when Mike was killed and Chris heard the news, he contacted her himself and set up a meeting. It was the start of many such meetings, encouraged by Mrs Roland, and now, nine months later, their business was established and beginning to make the headway Liz had predicted.

Thinking of Liz, Cassandra realised she ought to give her a ring and thank her for lunch the previous day. Liz's work, on a famous women's magazine, entailed many such lunches, but for Cassandra it had been a less familiar experience. Lunches generally were spent at her desk, with a sandwich from the local delicatessen, and the chance to open the windows in Chris's absence, and get rid of a little of the smoke haze. Chris usually went to the pub round the corner, eating his sandwiches with a pint and exchanging news with the staff from the hospital across the street. It was a popular meeting place, but although she was often invited to join him, Cassandra preferred to keep their association on a business footing.

As usual, Chris left the office at about a quarter to one, but after he had gone Cassandra felt curiously restless. Somehow the idea of sitting here enjoying a solitary sandwich had no appeal, and on impulse she got up from her chair and went to put on her jacket. It was a cold day, but sunny, and she decided to take a cab to Fetter Lane and surprise Liz. If she was free, they might have lunch together. If not, at least it would give her a break.

A car drove into the mews as she was descending the iron staircase, her heels clattering on the hollow slats. It was a dark green car, low and powerful-looking, and as she halted uncertainly, a man thrust open the door and climbed out.

It was Jay Ravek. There was no mistaking his lean indolent grace, or the silky hair that persisted in falling over his forehead. In a pair of dark pants and a corded jacket, his dark silk shirt opened at the neck in spite of the cold, he exhibited all the magnetism and sexuality she remembered, and just looking at him, she could feel every inch of her skin tingling.

He stood after closing the car door, inspecting his surroundings, and Cassandra guessed he was looking for her office. For an anxious moment she didn't know what to do. He hadn't seen her, that much was obvious, and she knew a ridiculous impulse to rush back up the steps and lock the door, before he noticed her. But that would have been silly and childish, and besides, she was taking it for granted he was coming to see her. He might not be, and in any case she was on her way out. Even so, it took a certain amount of courage to continue on down the steps as if she hadn't recognised him, when every step she took seemed to echo horribly in the quiet mews.

He heard her at once, and the dark eyes she remembered so well fastened on her slender figure, his mouth curving into a wry smile as he came towards her.

'Mrs Roland,' he acknowledged her easily, as she reached the cobbled yard. 'This is a coincidence. I was just coming to see you.'

'You were?' Cassandra assumed a cool smile of enquiry.

'Yes.' He inclined his head. Even in her heeled boots he was taller than she was, and it gave him a slight advantage. 'Didn't your mother-in-law tell you? I tried to phone you last night.'

Cassandra thought quickly. 'It—er—it's Mr Ravek, isn't it?' she exclaimed, ignoring his mildly incredulous intake of breath. 'Why, yes. Yes, Thea did say something about a call.'

Jay Ravek's eyes revealed his scepticism. Looking into their definitely mocking depths, Cassandra was left in no doubt as to his disbelief in the part she was playing, and remembering how his name had slipped out the day before, perhaps he could not be blamed for that.

Wanting—*needing*—to restore her credibility, Cassandra hastened on: 'I was just going to lunch, but if there's anything we can do for you, perhaps you could come back——'

'I was hoping to persuade you to have lunch with me,' he interrupted her smoothly, and the frankness of his approach left her briefly speechless.

'You—were hoping——' she got out, when she was able to drag sufficient air into her lungs, and once again he took the initiative.

'Yes.' He glanced round at his car. 'I was reliably informed that you didn't usually go out for lunch, but it seems my informant was mistaken.'

The hooded dark eyes were on her again, mildly amused now but interrogative, mocking her belief that she could handle any situation. She felt he could see right through her, and through any little ploy that she might use. He was not like Mike. He was not like any man she had known before. He was a totally new experience.

'Was he?' he asked at last.

'Was he—what?' She felt disorientated.

'Was my informant wrong? Do you normally go out to lunch?'

Cassandra took a deep breath. 'Why did you ring me, Mr Ravek? What do you really want?'

'You,' he declared, without scruple, and as her eyes widened with incredulity, he added: 'But first I must apologise if I've caused you any embarrassment. I had no idea you and your mother-in-law lived in the same building.'

She gazed at him. 'I don't see the relevance.'

'Don't you?' He shrugged. 'No, well, perhaps not. You are in business, after all. You must get a lot of calls.'

She drew a deep breath. 'Is this business, Mr Ravek?'

His mouth turned down. 'I think you know better than that.'

Cassandra gasped. 'Are you always so direct?'

'Would you prefer a different kind of approach?'

She shook her head. 'It's not something I'm familiar with,' she said blankly. 'Mr Ravek——'

'Jay,' he corrected her briefly. Then: 'Look, it's too cold to talk here. Do you have an appointment, or will you let me buy you lunch?'

Cassandra shivered, suddenly becoming aware of her surroundings again. 'I don't think——'

'Why not?' His lean face revealed a trace of irritation. 'You know you shouldn't believe everything you read in the press.'

'I don't.' That much was true. But Liz had been so vehement. 'I just——'

'What harm can eating lunch with me do?' he interposed swiftly. 'I don't bite, and I do know my table manners!'

Cassandra half smiled. 'I'm sure you do.'

'Is that a grudging acceptance?'

She made a decision. 'All right.'

'Good.' He gestured towards his car. 'Shall we go?'

Her determination wavered. Her impulsive consent to eat with him had not taken into account the method of getting to a restaurant, and somehow his car seemed such an intimate form of transport after what he had said. After all, what did she know about this man? Nothing that was good, certainly.

He seemed to sense her uncertainty, however, and his expression twisted into an ironic smile. 'You can trust me,' he said flatly. 'I promise I won't do anything you don't want me to do. Now, can we get moving?'

Cassandra gave in, and at her nod of acquiescence, Jay Ravek swung open the nearside door of the vehicle and waited while she got inside. His own entry was accomplished with the ease of long practice, and after settling his length behind the wheel, he started the engine.

As they turned out of the mews, Cassandra spared a thought for Chris, realising she should have left him a message telling him where she was going. But to suggest doing so now would smack of over-caution, and she could well imagine Jay Ravek's interpretation of her leaving some explanatory note.

The car was soon bogged down in the lunchtime snarl-ups, and feeling the need to clarify her position, Cassandra endeavoured to make light conversation.

What he had said earlier, about his reasons for ringing her, didn't seem credible somehow, and linking her hands together in her lap, she introduced the usual topics of weather and traffic.

His responses were monosyllabic as he concentrated on negotiating the busy streets, but once they had a clear stretch of road, he cast a lazy glance in her direction.

'You knew I'd ring, didn't you?' he remarked, disturbing her anew. 'What did your mother-in-law tell you?'

Cassandra bent her head. 'Oh, only that you'd rung. As you said, she thought you were a client. Only most people ring the studio.'

'Most men?'

Cassandra looked up indignantly. 'Most clients,' she corrected him shortly, and Jay inclined his head.

'But you did know?'

Cassandra schooled her features. 'How could I?'

'I don't believe you're that naïve,' he responded, his voice low and disruptive. 'But——' he shrugged, 'we'll play it your way, if it suits you.'

Cassandra didn't know how to answer him, so she didn't try. Instead, she tried to guess where he was taking her, and what she was going to tell Chris when she got back.

Jay eventually turned the powerful sports car into the car park of a hotel north of Willesden. It was not a hotel Cassandra was familiar with, but judging by the number of cars in the parking area, it was a popular eating place.

A cocktail bar gave on to a small dining room, and mentioning that they could get a drink at their table, Jay preceded Cassandra into the restaurant. They were shown to a table at the far side of the room, overlooking the sunken garden at the back of the hotel, where wilting plants surrounded a murky rock pool.

A waiter provided menus, and Jay asked Cassandra what she would like to drink.

'Oh, just a dry Martini, please,' she answered politely, and he ordered a gin and tonic for himself before allowing the waiter to depart.

'So,' he said, when they were alone, 'do you feel happier now?'

Cassandra fingered the red napkin in front of her. 'I don't know this place,' she replied, without answering him. 'Do you come here often?'

Jay lay back in his chair, regarding her with sardonic eyes. 'I guess Liz Lester has been talking,' he remarked. 'What did she tell you?'

'Not a lot.' Cassandra kept her tone light, and forced herself to look at the menu. 'What do you recommend? I rather fancy scampi. How about you?'

'Food's not a fetish with me,' he responded easily, putting his menu aside. 'So long as it's reasonably cooked, a steak will do fine.'

Cassandra nodded, glad of the diversion from more personal matters. 'Yes,' she said, 'I like steak, too. But I think I'll stick to the fish. It sounds delicious.'

'Good.'

His acquiescence was indifferent and she was glad when the waiter brought their drinks, and she was able to use her glass as a barrier between them. His eyes were too penetrating, his perception too shrewd; and she looked at the other diners in an effort to avoid looking at him, in case he could read her thoughts as well.

'I suppose you do a lot of entertaining,' he remarked at last, his voice lower, more persuasive. 'In the course of your—work, naturally.'

Cassandra turned her lovely eyes in his direction. She had the distinct suspicion there was an insult there somewhere, but for the life of her she couldn't understand why he should be baiting her in this way.

'I—we—do entertain, occasionally,' she agreed, shaking her head when he offered her another drink. 'But the company is very small yet. We don't have an unlimited expense account.'

'No.' He rested his arms on the table, cradling his glass between his palms. 'And there's just the two of you—you and this young man, Chris Allen?'

'Yes.'

The waiter came to take their order, and after he was gone again, Jay continued his catechism: 'Have you known him long? Allen, I mean?'

Cassandra shrugged. 'About seven years, I suppose. I knew him before—before I was married.'

'Ah——' Jay absorbed this with a curious expression. 'Perhaps you should have married him. You might have been—happier.'

She held up her head. 'Maybe,' she responded, her tone a little chilly now, and as if realising she was beginning to resent his interrogation, Jay smiled.

'I guess you're wondering why you agreed to have lunch with such an ignorant swine, aren't you?' he suggested ruefully. 'Forgive me, but——' he paused, 'perhaps I'm not used to such sensitive companionship.'

Cassandra hesitated. 'I should have thought that was patently untrue,' she declared steadily, and his lean mouth took on a humorous twist.

'So I was right—Liz has been talking. Am I allowed to say anything in my own defence?'

She sighed, putting down her glass, not quite sure whether to take him seriously or not. 'You don't have to defend yourself to me, Mr Ravek,' she stated carefully. 'The way you conduct your affairs is no concern of mine.'

It sounded abominably smug, but he seemed not to take offence, and the arrival of the waiter with their soup prevented any further intimate conversation. Much to her relief, the next twenty minutes were taken up in this way and Cassandra was free to concentrate on the meal and evade any further searching questions. But, inevitably, after she had refused a dessert, coffee was served, and gaining her permission to light a long, narrow cheroot, Jay resumed his cross-examination.

'Suppose,' he said, attracting her unwilling attention, 'suppose I wanted to make it your concern; the way I conduct my affairs, I mean.' His eyes narrowed, dark and sensual between the thick lashes. 'Does it matter to you how many women there've been in my life?'

'I—why——' Cassandra controlled her colour with the greatest difficulty. 'Mr Ravek——'

'Jay!'

'—are you trying to insult me?'

'No.' He rested his elbows on the table. 'Why should you think that?'

Cassandra moistened her lips. 'Perhaps I'm out of touch——'

'But not out of reach?'

'Mr Ravek——'

'Mrs Roland?' His eyes were mocking her now. 'You're an intriguing lady. I can't make up my mind whether you want to go to bed with me or not, and if the answer is no, what the hell am I doing here?'

Cassandra remained in her seat mainly because she doubted her legs would carry her across the room. But her face was red with embarrassment now, and anger at his outrageous statement far outweighed the attraction she had felt towards him.

'Do you only take a female out to lunch if you think she wants to go to bed with you?' she demanded, in a low angry voice, and his mocking smile briefly lit the dark contours of his face.

'In these circumstances, is it so surprising?' he countered, drawing on his cheroot. 'Don't look so shocked, Mrs Roland. It's a little late for that, don't you think?'

Cassandra could only assume the worst. Obviously,

he believed she had been warned about him, but had chosen to ignore the warning; and in essence it was true. But she had not truly taken everything Liz had told her as gospel, and in consequence, she was left to face this humiliating confrontation unprepared.

'I think I'd like to leave now, Mr Ravek,' she declared stiffly, glancing round, as if she hoped some stalwart knight in shining armour might come and rescue her. 'You've had your fun. Could you please ask the waiter to call a taxi for me.'

'That won't be necessary.' With an abrupt movement, he thrust back his chair and got to his feet.

His action brought the waiter to his side, and while he was attending to the bill, Cassandra took the opportunity to escape. She had no desire to drive back to the office with him, but when he emerged from the building, he found her thwarted, on the car park.

'I'd prefer to take a cab,' she declared, when he appeared, but Jay only moved his shoulders in an indifferent gesture.

'But as you can see, there aren't any,' he observed, his dark gaze sweeping the car park. 'Come on, I'll take you back. You can warm your cold feet in the Ferrari.'

Cassandra's blood boiled. 'You're despicable!'

'Yes, so I've been told,' he agreed, without rancour. 'Now, stop looking so outraged, and get in the car. Believe me, my ardour has been satisfactorily doused.'

If she hadn't felt so furious with him, Cassandra knew she could have seen the funny side of this. The trouble was, in spite of everything, he was still the most disturbing man she had ever met, and if he had not made her feel so insignificant, she might well have given into his sensual attraction.

To her relief, Chris had not returned when she got back to the office, and glancing at her watch she was amazed to discover it was only a little over an hour since she had left. Somehow it had seemed so much

longer than that, and her face was still burning as she
seated herself at her desk.

Jay had not spoken on the journey back to the studio,
and after depositing her in Chandler Mews, he had
driven away without a backward glance. She wondered
what he was thinking, what interpretation he had put
on her behaviour, and wished she understood herself
what it was she really wanted.

By the time Chris came back, she had herself reasonably in control, but the bright flags of colour in her
cheeks attracted his attention.

'You look busy,' he remarked, no doubt imagining
the heat she was displaying was due to honest toil.
'Didn't you go and get a sandwich? Don't start missing
meals. You're just beginning to lose that lean and
hungry look.'

'Well, thanks!' Cassandra tried to adopt a humorous
tone. 'I'll bear that in mind when I'm tipping the scales.'

'There's no fear of you doing that,' he retorted, lighting the inevitable cigarette. But then, with unexpected
perception, he added: 'You haven't been having a fight
with somebody, have you? You look a bit hot and
bothered.'

'I forgot to open the windows,' replied Cassandra,
hiding behind the hornrims of her spectacles. 'Did you
have a pleasant time at the Black Swan? I don't know
how you can eat pies every day of the week.'

'Oh, I vary them with sandwiches,' Chris answered
airily, taking his seat and picking up his pencil. 'And if
you'd ever tasted June's cooking, I guarantee you'd
welcome the change.'

Cassandra's laughter was not forced. 'You exagger-
ate,' she exclaimed. 'Nowadays, anybody can learn to
defrost a beefburger or put a tray of chips in the oven.'

'Want to bet?' Chris grinned across at her. 'So—why
don't you invite me round to your flat and show me
how a proper meal should taste?'

Cassandra looked at him for a moment, then shook her head, bending over her desk. 'You'd better finish off that layout for the kitchen,' she said, avoiding any further complications. 'I want to drive down to the house tomorrow afternoon, and I'd like to take the designs with me.'

'Okay.'

Chris shrugged, taking his dismissal without rancour. They had had many such exchanges since they began to work together, and so far Cassandra had found no difficulty in keeping their relationship on an impersonal basis. But she couldn't help wondering how he would react if she told him what Jay Ravek had said to her, and while the inclination to avail herself of his sympathy was attractive, she knew she could be inviting a far more explosive situation.

The telephone rang in the middle of the afternoon and she let Chris answer it, stiffening when he held the receiver out to her. 'That man,' he mouthed, frowning at her look of consternation. 'You know—the accountant I told you rang this morning.'

'Oh!' Cassandra's sigh of relief aroused a look of curiosity in Chris's eyes, but he said nothing, just handed over the receiver, and resumed his calculations as she spoke into the mouthpiece.

'Mrs Roland?' Paul Ludlum's voice was young and attractive. 'I hope I'm not ringing at an awkward time, but I did ring you earlier.'

'I know, and I'm sorry I didn't answer your call.' Cassandra was contrite. 'I—er—it's been quite a hectic day.'

She made a face at Chris's disbelievingly raised eyebrows, and listened with assumed concentration to what the accountant had to say. Obviously, the fact that his father and Mike's had been friends gave a certain partiality to his tone, and in spite of her misgivings, he seemed to think she could well afford professional advice.

'I'd like to call and look over your books,' he ventured at last. 'When would that be convenient? I don't want to interfere with your working schedules.'

'Oh——' Cassandra shrugged her shoulders, and put her hand over the mouthpiece so that she could speak privately to Chris. 'He wants to come and look at the books,' she said, looking anxious. 'Do you really think it's a good idea?'

'Sure,' Chris nodded. 'Tell him to come tomorrow, while you're down at Windsor. I guess I could manage to show him round.'

Cassandra nodded. 'Oh, good.' She removed her hand, and spoke to Paul Ludlum again. 'Would tomorrow morning be all right?'

'Tomorrow morning? Yes, I think I could manage that. Around eleven?'

'Around eleven,' Cassandra repeated in agreement, then rang off before she could change her mind.

'What's your problem?' Chris demanded, as she chewed unhappily on the end of her pencil. 'We're going to need an accountant, Cass. You can't keep on burning the candle at both ends.'

'Hardly that,' she grimaced.

'No. But you do work in the evenings, when you should be out enjoying yourself.'

'Oh, yes?' Cassandra was sardonic. 'Chris, I don't honestly think I was cut out for enjoying myself.'

'What rubbish!' Chris was impatient. 'Look, just because Mike made your life a misery——'

'Let's not talk about that, Chris.'

Cassandra interrupted him, but Chris was determined to be heard. 'Why not?' he demanded. 'I know he's dead, and you don't want to say bad things about him, but let's face it—he wasn't the man to make you happy.'

Cassandra went to plug in the kettle. 'Maybe it was my fault,' she mumbled, her back to him, smarting from the remembrance of her lunch with Jay Ravek. 'Maybe I don't—well——'

'Well—what?'

'I don't know.' She sighed. 'Maybe I attract the wrong kind of men.'

'What——' muttered Chris, swearing under his breath, but Cassandra heard him and shook her head.

'I mean it. Perhaps the kind of man I really need isn't attracted to me.'

'Oh, Cass——'

'Well, why not?' She grimaced. 'I guess I give the wrong impression. Mike used to say that.'

Chris raised his eyes heavenward. 'Cass, you're a sexy lady——'

'I may look that way, but I'm not,' declared Cassandra firmly, her lips twitching a little at the incongruity of this conversation. 'Honestly, Chris, I don't think I'm cut out for—well, for that kind of a relationship. I thought I was—but I was wrong.'

CHAPTER THREE

Two days later the weather changed. It had been cold and damp, but not frosty, however, when Cassandra awakened on Friday morning, it was to find the roofs of the flats opposite were white with snow. It was very picturesque, if less so in the street below. The movement of cars and milk-floats, and the constant tramp of feet, had left a slushy mess that was anything but attractive, and she turned away from the window, wishing it was Saturday.

It had seemed an unusually long week, and she could only put it down to the poor nights she was having. Since Wednesday, and her abortive outing with Jay Ravek, she had been unable to relax, and she had been looking forward to the weekend and the chance to get out of London.

She was hoping to go up to Derbyshire, to stay with some friends of Mike's, but the forecast was not encouraging. There had been heavy falls of snow outside the London area and Derbyshire had been mentioned, so she prepared her breakfast resignedly, realising her trip might well have to be cancelled.

Her doorbell rang as she was eating a slice of toast, and going to answer it she found Mike's mother on the threshold. An attractive woman in her late forties, Thea Roland kissed her daughter-in-law warmly, and at her invitation entered the flat, accepting the offer of a cup of coffee.

'I came to see whether you're still planning to drive up to Matlock, darling,' she said, draping herself elegantly over the arm of the sofa. 'Have you heard the weather forecast? It's not good.'

'I know.' Cassandra poured her mother-in-law's coffee. 'I was just wondering what I should do.'

'Don't go,' declared Mrs Roland at once, accepting the cup Cassandra proffered. 'Darling, it would be madness to drive all that way! Besides, with the roads so bad, it wouldn't be worth it. You'd hardly get there before you had to come home.'

'Yes.' Cassandra bit her lip indecisively. 'And I was so hoping to get away.'

'Were you?' Mrs Roland regarded her speculatively for a moment. 'I thought you were looking a little tense last evening. Is anything wrong? Paul didn't turn his thumbs down or anything, did he?'

'Paul? Oh, you mean the accountant.' Cassandra shook her head. 'No. No, actually, he was rather optimistic.'

'I told you so!' Mrs Roland looked delighted. 'What did you think of him? I meant to ask you.'

'Well, I didn't meet him, as it happens,' Cassandra sighed. 'I had to go to Windsor. Chris handled it.'

'Did he? What a shame!' Mrs Roland's eyes twinkled. 'I rather hoped you'd approve of that young man.'

Cassandra gave a rueful smile. 'Oh, Thea! Not matchmaking again!'

'Why not?' Thea Roland was unabashed. 'Darling, you're so young. You mustn't let Mike's death influence you. You have plenty of time to marry again, and give me some grandchildren. Oh, yes,' this as Cassandra would have interrupted her, 'I shall consider your children my grandchildren. Just as I consider you the daughter I never had.'

Cassandra bent to hug the older woman. 'Thea, that's very sweet of you, but——'

'I know. You don't want to get married again.'

'Right.'

'You will.' Thea sounded confident. 'Oh, and by the way, did you ever get in touch with that man who rang on Tuesday evening? You remember—Jay Ravek?'

Cassandra took a deep breath. 'He—as a matter of fact he came to the studio on Wednesday.'

'Did he?' Thea looked intrigued.

'Yes.' Cassandra spoke offhandedly. 'Unfortunately I—we were unable to help him.'

'What a pity!' Thea was irrepressible. 'He sounded nice. Even if he does have quite a reputation.'

Cassandra turned away to clear the table of her dirty cup and plate. 'Well, I don't want to rush you, Thea, but——'

'I know—you have to go.' Thea got up obediently, and carried her cup through to the tiny kitchen. 'But you will reconsider going to Derbyshire, won't you, Cass? I shall worry terribly if you insist on taking the car.'

Cassandra hugged her again. 'I promise I'll give the matter careful consideration,' she said. 'I suppose I could always use the train.'

'You could go next weekend,' Thea declared, walking towards the door. 'But anyway, I'll probably see you this evening. You can tell me your decision then.'

'I will.'

Cassandra accompanied her to the door, and after she had gone, she ran a hasty comb through her hair and checked her make-up. Did she look pale? Did her disturbed nights show? She hated the idea that Jay Ravek could affect her in this way, when obviously she had no such reaction on him.

Liz rang in the middle of the morning, and Cassandra, apologising for not having rung her, wondered what Liz would say if she told her of that disastrous lunch with Jay Ravek. Of course, Liz would only say 'I told you so', but somehow, in spite of his insolence, Cassandra knew a curious reluctance to discuss Jay with her friend.

'I'm calling to see if you'd like to come to a party this

evening,' Liz went on, after the preliminaries were over.
'I know you said you were going up to Matlock this
weekend, but what with the snow and so on, I thought
you might be staying at home.'

'I am considering it,' Cassandra admitted, glancing
towards the windows, where a swirling snowstorm was
whitening the panes.

'I thought it was possible,' Liz agreed. 'I guessed you
wouldn't want to come if you were planning to leave
early tomorrow morning, but if you're not . . .'

'Where is the party?' Cassandra was hesitant. 'Who's
giving it?'

'I am,' Liz retorted with a laugh. 'Everyone seems to
be staying in town this weekend, and I thought it was a
good idea.'

'Hmm.' Cassandra was doubtful. Right now, the idea
of going to one of Liz's parties and meeting some of the
bright young men she usually had in tow was not appealing. She had had enough of men for the time being,
but she could hardly say that to Liz without running
into awkward explanations. Besides, perhaps some
innocuous company was exactly what she needed to
restore her confidence.

'Come on, Cass.' Liz was persuasive. 'Isn't your
mother-in-law always telling you you should get out
more?'

'Yes,' Cassandra sighed. 'All right. Why not? What
time?'

Later that evening, however, preparing to go out to
the party, she wished she had not been so malleable.
It was a bitterly cold evening, and the snow that had
fallen earlier had frozen, making the roads icy and dangerous.

Deciding what to wear was a problem, too. Liz's
parties were always informal, but the girls she invited
generally showed up in very sophisticated gear.
Cassandra's casual clothes were not sophisticated, and

her eventual choice was a jumpsuit of olive-green velvet, which would help to keep her warm, as well as looking attractive.

Liz's flat was in Knightsbridge, a rather select area, where the rents were far out of Cassandra's price range. But Liz had a very good job, as well as having a private income from her parents, and money had never been a problem with her.

The Alfasud's wheels spun on the slippery road as Cassandra drove across town. Any sudden acceleration caused the tyres to lose purchase, and by the time she reached Carlton Square her arms were aching. There were already a number of cars parked around the snow-covered stretch of turf from which the cul-de-sac got its name, but she managed to squeeze the Alfa between an M.G. and a Mercedes. With a feeling of relief she got out of the car, locked it, and crunched across the frozen ridges of snow to the lighted entrance of Dower Court.

Liz's flat was on the first floor of the house. Built in Victorian times, Dower Court had once been a family house, but latterly it had been converted into four flats, each occupying one of the three floors and the basement. In consequence, the flats were large and spacious, and throwing a party in the huge living room was no problem at all.

Bettina, Liz's housemaid, opened the door to her ring, and entering the flat Cassandra was surprised anyone had heard her above the din that was going on. A tape deck was vibrating the ceiling, and the constant sound of voices swelled above the throbbing beat of electric guitars. Cassandra had once asked Liz whether her neighbours didn't object to the noise, but Liz's airy retort had been that she invited all the neighbours for that very reason, and in consequence no one could reasonably complain.

Bettina took Cassandra's coat and handed her a glass of champagne, before leaving her to make her own way into the throng. It was impossible to perform formal introductions when people gathered together in groups, and besides, those nearest the door had turned to see who it was, and Cassandra thankfully recognised a familiar face.

'Hi, Cass!' Jennie Ainsley was Liz's secretary, and they had met on several occasions at parties like this. 'You're late. Liz was beginning to think you weren't going to turn up. Come and join us!'

'Thanks,' Cassandra smiled, encompassing the group of people surrounding the younger girl. Richard Jeffries, Liz's editor, was there, as well as one or two younger men, and Pamela Shaftesbury, who also worked for the magazine. 'The roads are so bad,' she explained ruefully. 'It took twice as long as it normally does.'

'You've driven over?' Richard looked surprised.

'Well, it's so hard to get a taxi later,' Cassandra agreed. 'Besides, I didn't realise it was freezing so hard until I almost collided with a bus!'

'I walked,' said Jennie, grimacing. 'It was easier than waiting for a bus. I only hope I find someone to take me home.'

Cassandra shared her laughter, and then Liz was beside them, her lips warm against Cassandra's cold cheek. 'Darling, you're here! I didn't see you. You should have told me.'

'I've only been here about five minutes,' explained Cassandra apologetically. 'It was pretty hairy driving. Jennie was just saying she walked.'

'You should have taken a cab,' declared Liz, linking her arm and drawing her away from the group. 'Come on, I have someone I want you to meet. You remember I told you about Dave Adams?'

It was a pleasant way to spend an evening, Cassandra reflected later, as she helped herself to another chicken vol-au-vent. Now that she was here, she was not sorry she had come, and she had managed to avoid the escort

Liz had chosen for her. She had danced with several young men without becoming entangled with any of them, but now, with the lights lowered to offer a discreet intimacy, she thought it was safer to stay by the buffet tables.

'Dance with me?'

The quietly spoken invitation came from behind her, and she turned to make her refusal. 'I'm sorry,' she was beginning, 'but I don't——' when all the breath seemed to leave her lungs. The man standing behind her was disturbingly familiar, and remembering Liz's reactions to him, she half suspected she was hallucinating. But the cool breath that blew in her face was human, and so too were the cold fingers that curved round the nape of her neck.

'*You!*' she breathed, still half bemused by his appearance. 'What are you doing here? Did Liz invite you? I don't believe it! She wouldn't have done that. Not when——'

'Relax,' said Jay, drawing her towards him, and although inside she was protesting, she was too shocked to resist. 'Your friend is unaware of my presence at this moment. I gatecrashed. Does that answer your question? I wanted to speak to you.'

His last words seemed to bring Cassandra to an awareness of what she was doing, and her palms pressed insistently against the rough material of his jacket. He was not dressed for a party. His shirt was made of coarse cotton, and his jerkin was denim. As his hands slid down to her hips, compelling her against him, she guessed his pants were denim, too, the hardness of his thigh muscles pressing against her leg.

'I think you should leave,' she whispered fiercely, not wanting to cause a scene, but unwilling to allow his intrusion to go unchallenged.

'If you'll come with me,' he conceded, looking down at her in the dim light, and in spite of herself Cassandra's pulses fluttered at the narrow-eyed sensuality of his gaze.

'I don't think so,' she said, dragging her eyes away from his face and concentrating instead on the un-buttoned neckline of his shirt. But the glimpse of fine body hair just visible above the opening made her senses tingle, and she stepped back from him abruptly, aware of an instinctive response.

It was the amount of alcohol she had drunk, she thought weakly, remembering the glasses of champagne she had swallowed on an empty stomach. Nevertheless, she could not deny the surge of excitement his appear-ance had engendered, and weakness, like a palsy, was invading her lower limbs.

'I wanted to apologise,' he said huskily, stepping near to her again, and although Cassandra moved her head from side to side, the press of people around them made it difficult for her to keep a distance between them.

'To me?' she queried, glancing anxiously about her, and his mouth slanted ruefully as he acknowledged her bitter scepticism.

'I didn't know,' he said, and now she looked up at him with evident perplexity. 'Did you hear what I said?' he demanded, bending his head so that his lips brushed her ear-lobe. 'I didn't know,' and in her agitated state she was almost prepared to swear his tongue touched her skin. 'No one bothered to tell me that your husband was dead!'

Cassandra blinked. 'But—you must have known——'

'No.' He shook his head.

'You rang my mother-in-law's flat!'

'Exactly.' His eyes were disturbingly intent. 'When I found the number in the directory, I naturally assumed you must be divorced. It's listed in your mother-in-law's name,' he explained. 'When she told me you had a flat in another part of the building, I inferred you were still living with your husband.'

'Did you?' As his hands curved over her shoulders, flexing against the soft pile of the velvet, Cassandra strove to retain her detachment. 'Yet you still came to the office the next day—you still asked me to have lunch with you!'

'I know it.' His thumb brushed sensuously against her jawline, and the room seemed suddenly lacking in air.

'It—it didn't bother you,' she persisted, her voice annoyingly husky. 'My being married, I mean.' She took a deep breath, and went on: 'I'd heard you had no scruples about getting what you wanted.'

Jay's mouth twisted. 'Someone's done a good job of crucifying my character.' His eyes darkened. 'Believe it or not, but I have never attempted to break up anyone's marriage.'

'You have been involved with married women,' Cassandra accused him tensely, shivering as his finger probed the collar of her suit. 'I suppose you're going to say they were to blame!'

'No.' Jay's hand slid behind her head, tangling in the silvery blonde waves that wrapped themselves treacherously about his fingers. 'But they knew what they were doing.'

'That's very convenient, isn't it?' Cassandra shifted her head, but she couldn't free herself. 'I suppose it didn't occur to you that their husbands might have objected!'

Jay expelled his breath heavily, his lean features suddenly grimly etched in the subtle lighting of the room. 'Look,' he said, and his voice was harsher than she had heard it, 'I didn't come here to discuss my indiscretions. I came to find you, to apologise, which I have, and now I want to get out of here and I want you to come with me.'

'Why should I?' Cassandra was stubbornly insistent. 'You think this excuses you? You—you were rude—and insulting—and nothing you can say can alter that.'

'Don't you want to know why I was rude and insulting?' he demanded, forcing her head back so that she had to look up at him. 'Hell, I don't do this kind of thing for fun! As it happens, I've never done it before.'

'You expect me to believe you——'

'I don't give a—if you believe me!' he retorted, using a word Cassandra had last heard in Mike's vocabulary. 'God, I don't even know why I came here! This really isn't my scene.'

'So why don't you go?' she countered, wincing as his fingers were tugged out of her hair. 'I don't know how you found me. I can't believe Liz would give you that information.'

'She didn't. Your mother-in-law did,' stated Jay roughly.

'Thea!' Cassandra gazed at him. 'You went to see Thea?'

'If that's your mother-in-law's name, yes.' He moved his shoulders dismissingly. 'I wanted to ask her your address. She explained that you weren't home.'

Cassandra understood now. She could imagine Thea's reaction to such an attractive male. It was typical of her to act first and ask questions afterwards.

Now she linked her fingers together and said tightly: 'I'm sorry, but you've had a wasted journey.'

'Have I?' He pushed his hands into the pockets of his jerkin. 'Don't you accept my apology?'

'Your apology comes a little late,' declared Cassandra firmly. 'You'd better go, before Liz sees you.'

'Believe it or not, I don't much care if Liz sees me,' he retorted shortly. Then: 'At least, see me off the premises.'

She hesitated. 'Oh—all right.'

As luck would have it, Liz was occupied at the other side of the room as they made their way to the door. Several people, particularly the girls present, gave Jay an interested appraisal as he passed, and Cassandra knew she would have to face some awkward questions when Liz heard of it. Still, she could honestly say she had not invited him, and the rest of the story need not be mentioned.

In the entry, away from prying eyes, she waited impatiently for him to leave. She would have opened the door for him, except that it would have looked too obvious. He would imagine she did not trust herself to be alone with him, which was both ridiculous and untrue. She had been married, for heaven's sake! Her experiences with Mike should have equipped her to deal with any situation. But she had to admit Jay Ravek was not like Mike, and his nearness was disruptive.

'Goodnight, then,' he said at last, removing his hands from his pockets.

'Goodnight.' Cassandra's response was stilted, and it was difficult to sustain an appearance of indifference when her emotions were so unstable. She was intensely aware of him, of the long brown fingers attaching the two sides of his jerkin, running the zip half up his chest, of his warm breath fanning her cheek, and the indefinable scent of his body. He checked his pockets, as if searching for his keys, and her eyes followed his movements with a helpless attention to detail. She didn't want to notice the fine gold chain around his neck or the slim gold watch on his dark wrist, but she couldn't seem to help it. The hair on his body, the brownness of his skin, disturbed her carefully schooled feelings, and most disturbing of all was her awareness of his maleness, taut against the skin-fitting tension of his pants. She couldn't seem to stop looking at him, and her mouth felt as dry as sand.

He was just a man, like any other man, she flayed herself inwardly, sweating with the effort to remain immune to his appeal. But no man had ever made her so aware of herself or aroused the desire to change her emotionally-starved existence.

'What's your name?' he asked suddenly, and she realised while she had been lost in thought he had reduced the space between them. 'Your mother-in-law called you—Cass? Is that right?'

'Cassandra, actually,' she got out unsteadily, and he smiled.

'Cassandra,' he repeated slowly. 'Apollo's Trojan princess. What do you prophesy for us, I wonder?' and as if unable to resist the temptation, he lifted his hand and trailed his knuckles down her cheek.

'Please——' she breathed, turning her head away from him, but the wall of the lobby was behind her, hard and unyielding.

'You do,' he countered softly, 'you do—please me,' and as she lifted her face helplessly, his mouth came down on hers.

It was not an aggressive assault, just a series of light compelling kisses, that released Cassandra's tension and caused her to respond. It was almost a relief to know what he intended, and the feather-light touch of his lips left her pliant and eager for more. It was almost a year since she had felt the caress of a man's mouth, and much longer than that since it was done with gentleness and sensitivity. Where was the harm? she thought, bemused by her own senses, so long as he went no further . . .

Jay was probing at her lips with gentle insistence, and although she had never enjoyed this kind of intimacy with Mike, it seemed the most natural thing in the world for her to let him have his way. Immediately, his mouth opened to accommodate hers, and his hands cradled her face, holding her captive. It was a tantalising experience. She was leaning against the wall now, but although she could feel Jay's legs brushing hers, he did not allow his weight to rest against her. He seemed quite content to play with her mouth, his lips moving softly over hers, evoking a sensual reaction that robbed her of breath and incited her emotions.

As the minutes passed, however, she became aware of a rising sense of frustration. For the first time in her life she felt a curious craving deep inside her, a craving that ran like liquid fire through her veins. Jay's teasing kisses were only tormenting that need, and she knew she had to do something about it. With a little sound low in her throat, she lifted her hands and grasped his shoulders, fusing his mouth with hers.

The parted ardour of her lips, combined with the yielding softness of her body, evoked a shuddering response. With a groan, Jay yielded against her, and her senses swam dizzily as his mouth moved deeply over hers. His kisses were demanding now, hungry and passionate, and she wound her arms around his neck, her nails raking the silky hair at his nape.

When at last he tore his mouth from hers, it was to trail quick burning kisses across her cheek and down the delicate curve of her jawline. With his hands in the small of her back, sensuously stroking her spine, Cassandra could only give herself up to the exquisite sensations he was inspiring, her knees sagging weakly beneath his urgent assault.

The heavy throbbing of his heart and the pulsating heat of his loins made her fiercely aware of his arousal, and when she turned her lips against his neck, she found his skin was moist with perspiration. It was an unwelcome discovery. It reminded her too well of other occasions when her husband had turned to her because there was no one else. Mike's selfishness, his brutality, his egotism, had eventually destroyed any love she had ever felt for him, but she remembered his sweating lust and was chilled by it.

Yet, even as a sense of panic rose inside her, she knew that this time it was different. Mike had never aroused the emotions Jay was arousing. He had never taken the time to awaken her dormant sensuality, or evoked any desire to respond to him as she was responding to Jay. She had never known what it was to want a man, and although she was afraid that her needs could never be assuaged, it was more, so much more, than she had believed herself capable of feeling.

'I hope I'm not interrupting anything.' Liz's voice was half amused, half impatient, as if she resented the implication that they had abandoned her party in favour of this lobby. 'Cass, I've been looking everywhere for you. I knew it couldn't be true, when Jennie told me she saw you leaving.'

Cassandra, struggling desperately to reorientate herself, wondered if anyone but Liz could stand there and ignore the very obvious fact that she *was* interrupting something. She doubted anyone else would do such a thing, and with this thought came the troubled realisation that as yet Liz had not identified the man with her. Jay had his back to her, and no doubt he was the last person Liz would expect to see.

Jay, too, had stiffened at the drawling sound of Liz's voice. With a muffled imprecation he put his hands against the wall and pushed himself away from her, and Cassandra saw the mask of insolence slide down across his face. He was obviously preparing himself for Liz's angry reactions, and Cassandra knew a feeling of intense loathing for the scene which must surely follow. If only it could have been avoided, she thought, as he turned to face their hostess, and she closed her eyes for a fleeting moment and offered up a little prayer.

'Hello, Liz!'

Jay's casual greeting stole the moment of its thunder, but Cassandra, seeing the dawning fury in Liz's face, knew she would not let this incident pass unchallenged.

'Jay Ravek!' she gritted, casting a brief but killing glance in Cassandra's direction. 'What the hell are you doing in my apartment?'

'I—I invited him!' Cassandra stepped forward jerkily,

before Jay could reply. 'You—you always say bring a friend, don't you, Liz? And—and as Jay called me just after you did——'

Liz's blue eyes were hard as agate. 'Are you trying to tell me you've been seeing this louse, Cass?'

'Jealous?'

Jay's ironic interjection was quickly superseded by Cassandra's hasty explanation. 'I—we—had lunch together on—on Wednesday,' she averred a little breathily, keeping her eyes on Liz. 'Oh, please, don't be upset! I—I know what I'm doing.'

'Do you?' Liz was scornful.

'It isn't really anything to do with you, is it?' Jay inserted mildly, and Liz gazed at him with burning frustration, evidently torn between the urge not to alienate Cassandra and the equally strong desire to have him thrown out.

'We were just leaving anyway,' Jay remarked, brushing back the swathe of dark hair that had fallen across his forehead with combing fingers. 'Get your coat, Cass. I don't think we're welcome here.'

'Cass is.' Liz put a detaining hand on the girl's arm. 'Darling, you're not leaving, surely! It's only a little after ten!'

Cassandra looked at Liz, then at Jay, and finally back to Liz again. She was torn, too, torn by the knowledge that if she went with Jay she would be committing herself to an unknown destiny, and in spite of her earlier conviction that he was not like Mike, her cooling blood was more cautious. It was too soon, her common sense asserted. She had only known of his existence for four days, and their actual contact could be measured in hours—or minutes. What if she was wrong? Liz's feelings about him couldn't hurt her, but her own could. What if what had happened between them didn't happen again? Did she want that kind of sterile relationship outside of marriage any more than she had wanted it with Mike?

She turned to look at him again, and Jay's eyes mirrored his feelings. He thought she was letting Liz influence her, when her friend's reactions played little part in her uncertainties. Looking at him, aware of his physical attraction, remembering how he had made her feel only minutes before, she wanted to go with him; but something, some inner caution, some fear of what it might mean to her, held her back, made her wary, urged her to guard against compulsion.

'All right, Liz, I'll stay,' she conceded, and instantly resented the expression of smug satisfaction that spread over the other girl's features. As her eyes turned almost guiltily to Jay, she saw that he was already opening the door, and the words she might have spoken in mitigation were silenced as it slammed behind him.

CHAPTER FOUR

THEA took an interminably long time to open the door, and when she did it was obvious that Cassandra had got her out of her bed. She had dragged on her woolly dressing gown over her brushed nylon pyjamas, and her hair stuck comically through the hairnet she had worn to keep her rollers in place.

'Cass!' she exclaimed protestingly, blinking at her daughter-in-law. 'Is there anything wrong? Is the building on fire or something? Do you realise it's barely seven o'clock!'

'I know.' Cassandra entered her mother-in-law's flat, and waited for her to close the door. 'But I wanted to make an early start, and I thought I should see you before I left.'

'An early start?' Thea groped blankly for the couch, and sank down weakly on to its soft cushions. 'Darling, you're not trying to tell me you're going to Derbyshire after all!' She shook her head. 'But last night you assured me you'd changed your mind.'

'I had.' Cassandra paced restlessly about the room, slim and attractive in a green corded pants suit, the trousers tucked warmly into knee-length leather boots. 'But,' she moved her shoulders jerkily, 'it's a fine morning, and the forecast is good for the rest of the day.'

Thea gazed at her disbelievingly. 'The roads are still bad, Cass. There hasn't been a thaw. Don't you think you're being foolhardy in attempting such a journey?'

'I need the break,' declared Cassandra tautly, linking her fingers together. 'I'm not a reckless driver, and I promise I'll take great care. I'll ring you as soon as I get to Matlock, honestly.'

Thea gathered the lapels of her dressing gown together, still looking worried. 'Cass, I don't understand you. Why, when you went off to Liz's party last evening, you said you'd rung Val and David and cancelled your weekend.'

'I had.' Cassandra spoke carelessly. 'But I can change my mind, can't I? They'll have no objection. They're not like that.'

Thea sighed. 'Well, I can't say I approve, Cass. It wouldn't be so bad if you were going with somebody. But alone!'

'I'll be all right.' Cassandra came to the couch and bent to kiss her mother-in-law's cheek. 'I'll see you Sunday evening, right? About nine.'

Thea got to her feet as Cassandra walked towards the door. 'Very well, if you're determined.' She made a helpless gesture. 'Do be careful.'

'I will.' Cassandra forced a smile and stepped out into the corridor.

'Oh, by the way——' Thea's unexpected summons halted her.

'Yes?'

'That man came here last night looking for you—Jay Ravek. I gave him Liz's address. Did you see him?'

'Er——' Cassandra wet her dry lips nervously. 'Er—yes. Yes. He turned up about nine o'clock.'

Thea grimaced. 'I hope you didn't mind my telling him where you were, but he said he knew Liz, so I was sure it would be all right.'

'Oh—oh, yes. Yes, of course.' Cassandra was purposely vague, but Thea wasn't quite finished yet.

'He's very attractive, isn't he?' she persisted, shivering a little as the cool draught of air from the corridor penetrated the open doorway. 'Did he bring you home?'

'Heavens, no!' Cassandra hid her clenched knuckles behind her back. 'Look love, I really ought to be going——'

'Yes.' Thea looked thoughtful. 'He's not the reason for this sudden decision to leave town, is he, Cass?'

'No!' Cassandra exhaled nervously. 'I've told you, Thea, I need the break.'

'But from what?' remarked her mother-in-law drily, and Cassandra made her escape before any more awkward questions were forthcoming.

It had been hard enough stalling Liz the night before. After Jay's peremptory departure, she had demanded to know how Cassandra had chanced to meet him again, and it had not been easy explaining about his visit to the studio.

'So you had lunch with him,' she declared tautly, her blue eyes cold and challenging, and Cassandra's flushed confirmation had met with an angry accusation.

'I told you what he was like,' she exclaimed. 'I warned you! God knows what might have happened just now, if I hadn't come looking for you!'

At this point, Cassandra's pride had reasserted itself. 'What could have happened?' she demanded hotly, a feeling of resentment swelling her determination not to be treated like a child. 'He was hardly likely to try and make it in the lobby of your flat!'

Liz changed her tactics and gave an offended sniff. 'Well, I'm sorry if you feel I'm interfering. I only want what's best for you, Cass, you know that.'

'Oh, Liz!' Cassandra was meant to—*and did*—feel a heel. 'Look, let me make my own mistakes, okay? I should be old enough to know better. But if I do fall flat on my face, then you're quite at liberty to say "I told you so"!'

'I just don't want you to get hurt, that's all.' Liz's concern was touching, and Cassandra felt contrite for lying to her in the first place. Yet what else could she have said? She could hardly allow Jay to be accused of gatecrashing, when she had so obviously been the reason for him still being there.

As luck would have it, their conversation was broken up at this point by the sudden influx of several more guests. They had obviously been partying elsewhere before coming on here, and in the general noise and confusion Cassandra was able to make herself scarce. In all honesty, she would have preferred to go home, and only the faint possibility that Jay might be sitting outside in his car, waiting for her to do just that, kept her where she was for another two hours. Surely it was too cold for anyone to wait that long, and to her relief when she finally went down to her car, there was no one about to molest her.

Now, in the grey light of dawn, she drove up the ramp from the basement garage and had her first taste of how slippery the roads still were. Even though the ramp had been salted the night before, the frequent passage of cars had melted most of it away, and her wheels spun uselessly at the first attempt.

Once out of Russell Place, however, she became more optimistic. The main thoroughfares in the city were almost free of ice, and she made good time in the quiet early traffic. Making for the North Circular Road, she was looking forward to getting on to the motorway, but she switched on the car radio to get an update on the weather report.

What she heard was not encouraging. Drivers were being warned that there was more heavy snow spreading from the north-west, and they were advised not to attempt any journey that was not absolutely necessary.

'Rubbish,' muttered Cassandra impatiently, glancing up at the distinctly overcast appearance of the sky. The motoring associations always looked on the black side, mainly to save themselves from being called out, she decided uncharitably.

Nevertheless, the traffic news that followed the weather report did give her food for thought. It transpired that the junction of the M.1 which she had hoped to use was closed, owing to several accidents, and motorists were being diverted via Barnet and Potters Bar. It seemed the best plan for her was to use the old A.1 trunk road, in the faint hope that she might be able to rejoin the M.1 at a later stage.

Of course, the diversion added miles to the journey, and beyond Stevenage, the dual carriageway narrowed to a single stream of traffic, with piles of snow heaped at the sides of the road. It was going to get worse, she thought unhappily, but still she pressed on, driven by the need to get right away from London.

She knew Thea had been right. Jay Ravek was behind this sudden urge to run. But it was crazy! What was she running from? After last night's episode, she had few illusions that she would see him again. She had had to choose, and she had remained with Liz. However much he might be attracted to her, he would not forgive her for that.

So why was she here, driving in appalling conditions, miles from her home and the people who cared about her? She felt so mixed-up and confused, she hardly needed a reason. But perhaps it was because she was afraid of what *she* might do, if Jay made no attempt to contact her. And that was really the crux of the matter. She didn't want to get that involved with anyone. She had wanted a relationship, yes, but not an obsession, and last night Jay had made her aware of how vulnerable she was where he was concerned. Perhaps what she had told Chris had been the truth: she simply attracted the wrong kind of men.

The signpost for Cambridge caught her attention. Just a few miles off to the east, and near enough to London not to create any problems driving back tomorrow. Why didn't she stay there overnight, find a hotel, and treat herself to an unexpected flavour of luxury? She could ring her mother-in-law from the hotel and explain what she was doing, then drive home again tomorrow afternoon.

The decision made, she indicated her intentions and turned off the dual carriageway. Immediately the road deteriorated into a slushy track. It was still early, and although there had been some traffic on the road, snow-flakes were already fluttering down again, covering the unsightly sludge and rapidly obscuring the signposts.

She had made her decision just in time, she reflected anxiously, as the snow thickened and the car's wind-screen wipers made heavy work of keeping it clear. If it was snowing like this in London, Thea would be worry-ing herself sick about her, and she began to feel rather selfish for having insisted on coming away.

She crawled into Cambridge soon after eleven, having taken fully an hour to cover the last ten miles. But once again the skies were clearing, even though it was still bitterly cold, and the blue sky overhead was a fitting backcloth to the spires of the ancient university city.

She parked near the city centre, and then, pulling on her hooded sheepskin coat over the jacket of her pants suit, she got out of the car and locked it, and walked towards the shopping precinct.

After a warming cup of coffee in a bar almost ex-clusively occupied by students she emerged, pink-cheeked, to look for a hotel. She scarcely looked older than a student herself, and the bold stares and ribald comments her presence had provoked had made her wish she'd been more circumspect in choosing her choice of venue.

She walked along St John's Street and stood for a while on Magdalene Bridge, looking down into the fast flowing waters of the River Cam. Even at this time of year there were still visitors willing to stand on the bridge and survey the various colleges, but Cassandra was glad she was no longer a student. It was much more satisfying to work for herself, to see the results of her labours in much more practical forms.

When the skies clouded over again, a grey reflection

in the water, she turned and walked back to the city centre, and the welcoming warmth of the King's Arms Hotel. She chose it simply because she liked the look of it, and its low beams and narrow staircases more than lived up to her anticipations.

The room she was given overlooked the Arts Theatre, and although it was not large, it was reasonably comfortable and deliciously warm. The central heating was not appropriate to its surroundings, but it was efficient, and she sank down on to the bed gratefully after the porter had left her. She had still to collect her car from the car park, but she could do that after lunch, and the porter had assured her that he would find a place for it in the yard at the back.

With only a momentary hesitation, she reached for the telephone and gave Thea's number to the operator. Then, waiting for it to be connected, she shed her coat and stretched out lazily on the bed. Let it snow, she thought indifferently, watching the huge flakes drifting past the window. She was snug and warm here, and for twenty-four hours she refused to contemplate the future.

When Thea's voice came on the line, it sounded incredibly far away. 'Hello?' she said tautly, almost as if she expected the worst, and Cassandra's sense of wellbeing evaporated abruptly as she realised how her mother-in-law must be feeling.

'Thea,' she said, lifting her voice slightly to compensate for the poor line. 'Thea, it's me, Cass. I just wanted to tell you all is well.'

'Cass! Cass, where are you?' Thea's voice rose accordingly. 'Oh, darling, I've been so worried about you. It's done nothing but snow since you left.'

'I know. It's the same here.'

'But where's here?' Thea sounded anxious. 'Cass, you can't have reached Matlock already. I just don't believe it.'

'Calm down. I haven't.' Cassandra drew a deep breath. 'I'm in Cambridge.'

'Cambridge?'

'Yes, Cambridge.' Cassandra sighed. 'I decided you were right after all and turned back, but I'm spending tonight in this hotel.'

'A hotel?' Thea gave a troubled exclamation. 'Cass, you haven't had an accident, have you? The car hasn't broken down or anything?'

'No, no, nothing like that.' Cass endeavoured to reassure her. 'Only as I'd planned to come away anyway, it seemed a bit pointless to drive straight back to town.'

'But why Cambridge? You don't know anyone there, do you?'

'No.' Cassandra conceded the point. 'But it's a place I've often wanted to visit, and the King's Arms is very nice and olde-worlde, and comfortable.'

'The King's Arms? That's the hotel where you're staying?'

'That's the one.' Cassandra moved her shoulders helplessly. 'You can ring me back if you don't believe me. Honestly, Thea, I'm fine.'

'No, no, I believe you.' Thea sounded simply worried now. 'I just wish I was there with you. I don't like you staying in a strange place alone.'

'Oh, honestly——' Cassandra exhaled impatiently. 'Thea, I'm not a baby. I can look after myself. Why is it people persist in treating me like an innocent abroad? I'm not. I know what I'm doing. And now I'm going to enjoy some lunch before spending the afternoon sightseeing.'

'But it's snowing, Cass!'

'I won't melt,' retorted Cassandra shortly, and rang off before she was tempted to say something stronger.

The dining room of the King's Arms was small and intimate, a huge log fire giving off the scent of burning wood. There were horse brasses on the walls, and various hunting trophies, and the buffet tables in the entrance groaned beneath the weight of cold meats and salads.

Cassandra chose a hot meal, and seated by the leaded windows with an uninterrupted view of the street outside, she had soup, and roast beef, and apple pie with custard. It was the first meal she had enjoyed for days, and she wasn't overly troubled by the occasionally speculative glances that were cast in her direction. The dining room had soon filled up, and she guessed it was a popular eating place at weekends. But to her relief, no one came to join her table for two, and she finished the meal with coffee before leaving the restaurant.

The afternoon took longer to fill than she had imagined. After a brisk walk to the car park, she drove the Alfa back to the hotel yard, and deposited her overnight bag in her room. Then, as the snow had not abated and a prolonged sightseeing excursion was out of the question, she spent a couple of hours looking round the shops, before going back to the hotel to watch television in her room.

The inevitable sporting programmes were of little interest to her, however, and the film on the alternative channel was too silly for words. Instead, she took out the book she had bought during her shopping spree, and applied herself determinedly to the exploits of its stalwart Georgian heroine.

'Jane Austen would turn in her grave if she knew,' she grimaced at last, throwing the book aside. For a supposedly well brought up young lady, the heroine of the drama had an unbecoming propensity for jumping into bed with every able-bodied man who took a fancy to her, and after reading of her panting surrender to the villain of the piece, Cassandra had had enough.

Leaving her chair, she walked to the windows, gazing down ruefully at the street below. It was after four-thirty, and in spite of the snow, darkness had fallen. Gradually the traffic was beginning to ease and people were hurrying home, and Cassandra knew an unwelcome sense of isolation at the thought of the evening ahead.

Turning away from the window, she surveyed her domain without enthusiasm. What could she do? She had little unpacking to trouble her. Apart from her nightdress and toiletries, she had only brought one dress with her, and she had hung that out earlier after she had collected the car. She could always take a bath or a shower, or simply hope there was something more inspiring on television, but somehow none of these alternatives held much in the way of entertainment.

With a sigh, she decided she would take a bath. She had fully three hours to fill before going down to dinner, and she seldom had time at home to enjoy a luxurious soak. With a feeling of relief at having come to a decision, she went into the adjoining bathroom and turned on the taps, before walking back to the bedroom to take off her clothes.

The hot water made her drowsy, and after the poor nights she had been having, it was no surprise that she found it difficult to keep her eyes open. It was so peaceful lying there, with only the muted sounds of the hotel to keep her company, and she lay back lazily, and made her mind a blank.

She must have dozed, because she awakened with a start to find the water had cooled considerably. She assumed that that was what had woken her, and with a little shiver, she climbed speedily out of the bath. She had obviously been foolish to linger in the water, and she chided herself impatiently for taking such a risk. If she had slipped and hit her head, she might have drowned, and she towelled herself vigorously to dispel the depressive influence of her thoughts.

Entering the bedroom again with a towel tucked

securely about her, she was glad of the welcoming warmth of the radiator. Her toes curled gratefully into the rough pile of the carpet, and in the dusky lamplight, the room had taken on an intimacy it had not previously displayed.

'You really shouldn't do that, you know.'

The shock of hearing a man's voice in a room she had believed to be empty caused her heart to race wildly. A scream rose unbidden to her throat, but her hand over her mouth silenced it as her visitor stepped out of the shadows.

'Sleep in the bath,' Jay continued irrepressibly, tucking his hands into the skin-hugging suede of his pants as he straightened away from the wall. 'Has no one ever warned you of the dangers?' His lips twitched. 'Not to mention the fact that you could drown.'

Indignation brought coherency: 'You mean—you saw me!' She clutched the towel convulsively. 'But—how——'

'How could I?' he anticipated her. 'It was quite easy really. You hadn't locked the door.'

'I meant how did you get in here?' she exclaimed resentfully. 'What are you doing here? And don't tell me it's coincidence!'

'I wouldn't insult your intelligence.' Jay moved his shoulders carelessly. 'Now, which answer would you like first? Why I'm here or how I got here?'

'I imagine you came by car,' retorted Cassandra icily. 'You know what I mean. How did you get into this room?'

'The porter let me in.'

'What?' Cassandra no longer felt cold. She felt hot and frustrated, and totally confused. 'I don't believe you. The porter wouldn't let a stranger in here.'

'Ah, but I'm not a stranger,' replied Jay, with an infuriating smile. 'I told him I was your husband. He was most understanding.'

'You did *what!*' Cassandra's legs felt decidedly unsteady. 'You told them—you had the nerve to pretend——'

'Calm down.' Jay's dark gaze appraised her evident upheaval, and belatedly Cassandra became aware of her revealing state of undress. 'If you'll let me explain, I'm sure you'll agree, I acted with your best interests at heart.'

'I doubt it.' Cassandra put up a nervous hand to her hair, feeling the moist tendrils curling against her nape. 'I think you should get out of here before I call the porter myself. I'm sure he'll take a pretty dim view of someone who forces his way into a woman's room without authority——'

'For God's sake, cool it, will you?' Jay gave her an impatient stare. 'I knocked but you didn't answer, even though they told me downstairs you were in. I was concerned——'

'Were you?'

'Yes, damn you, I was.'

'Well, that still doesn't explain what you're doing here,' exclaimed Cassandra tautly. 'Did you follow me?'

'If you mean did I hang about your flat all night waiting for you to make your appearance this morning, then no, I didn't follow you,' Jay retorted crisply. 'However, when your mother-in-law told me where you were——'

'Thea? Thea told you where I was?' Cassandra made a helpless gesture. 'Why would she do that? Did she telephone you?'

Jay sighed. 'No, she didn't telephone me.' He paused. 'I went round to your flat like you knew I would. And when I couldn't get any response, I used my initiative and contacted your mother-in-law again.'

'And she sent you here?' Cassandra felt terrible. 'Oh, she shouldn't have done that——'

'Will you stop jumping to conclusions?' Jay regarded

her impatiently. 'When she told me where you were, I was concerned. *We* were both concerned.'

Cassandra shook her head. 'There was no need to be. I—I intended driving to Matlock to see some friends. When the road conditions got bad, I came here.'

'You ran away,' he informed her flatly. 'From me.'

Cassandra gasped. 'You flatter yourself!'

'No, I don't. But I do know that what happened last night frightened you. God——' he scuffed his boot against the carpet, 'it frightened me.' He looked at her steadily. 'Believe me, I don't generally make this kind of running.'

Cassandra trembled. 'Am I supposed to take that as a compliment?'

'You can take it any way you like,' he replied huskily. 'Now, how about getting some clothes on, and we'll have dinner together.'

'You're staying?' Cassandra's lips parted.

'Would you have me drive back to town tonight?' He moved, and her body stiffened in anticipation of his touch, but all he did was draw back the curtain at the window to display the softly falling flakes. 'In that?'

Cassandra shrugged. 'I suppose not. But you can't stay here. Not at this hotel.'

'Why not?'

'Well, you know why not.'

'Ah——' He tilted his head. 'You don't want me to share your room.' He shrugged. 'No sweat. The hotel's not full, I can get a room of my own.'

Cassandra swallowed. 'But you told them we were married!'

'So what? Not all married couples share the same room.'

Cassandra sighed. 'I can't stop you.'

'Do you want to?'

Cassandra licked her dry lips. 'I—don't know.'

'That's promising anyway.' His smile returned as he

strolled towards the door. 'I'll leave you to get dressed. I'll meet you in the bar in—say, fifteen minutes?'

'Make it half an hour,' said Cassandra quickly, aware that she would need some time to recover her composure. He had come upon her unannounced, and he had disrupted what little detachment she had achieved. She would need a space to gather her scattered senses, and to recognise what might have happened if he had chosen to treat her differently. They were alone here. The staff of the hotel believed she was his wife. He could so easily have overpowered her, and remembering how he had observed her in the bath, she wondered if Liz would ever believe he had not tried to make love to her.

'Tell me something,' she said, as he reached the door, and he raised his dark brows in interrogation. 'Did— did Thea put you up to this?'

'Do you believe she could?' he enquired, with a wry twisting of his lips—and left her.

CHAPTER FIVE

THERE were fewer guests for dinner than there had been for lunch, due no doubt to the weather conditions. In consequence, the attention given to their table was obsequious, and Cassandra had difficulty in hiding her embarrassment every time Jay was addressed as *Mr* Roland.

Conversely, he seemed not to mind at all, his night-dark eyes meeting hers with lazy indulgence as he played his part to the full. She had not asked him what the receptionist had said when he went to book another room, but she could imagine the speculation his behaviour had evoked.

For her own part, she could not deny having prepared for the meal with a certain amount of anticipation. Brushing her hair until it curled in loving tendrils about her forehead, applying a rich tinted shadow to her lids to accentuate the green brilliance of her eyes, coating her lips with a matching lustre, she had been aware of a growing excitement. She even knew a sense of regret that she had no choice when it came to what dress she was going to wear, but the dipping cowl neck-line and wide raglan sleeves of the claret-coloured silk jersey looked reasonably acceptable to her critical eyes.

Now, sitting across from Jay at the table, she found her gaze drifting irresistibly in his direction. What was he thinking, she wondered? as he crumbled the roll on his plate. Why had he come after her? What did he want? And equally disturbing, what did she want of him?

It was difficult for her to assimilate her feelings. When her eyes lingered compulsively on the width of his shoulders, outlined beneath the dark blue suede of his jacket, she was made breathlessly aware of what he did to her. But it was this as much as anything that made her feel so insecure. She had wanted an affair, a casual relationship with no strings, that would rid her once and for all of the humiliating memories of her marriage to Mike Roland. But she was very much afraid she could not have that kind of relationship with Jay Ravek. In his own way, he could be equally destructive to her peace of mind.

She sighed, dragging her eyes away from him and tackling the smoked salmon she had ordered. She was not afraid of sex, she thought, her mind refusing to abandon its theme. She was not afraid of going to bed with a man, which in her experience was a vastly over-rated pastime. So what was there about Jay that made her wary? Surely her experiences with Mike had prepared her for any eventuality. It didn't make sense. She only knew that when Jay had kissed her the night before, she had hovered on the brink of a yawning chasm she had not known was there. Perhaps he was right. Perhaps she was afraid. But of what?

'I guess Liz thought I'd be annoyed when you chose not to leave with me last night,' Jay remarked suddenly, breaking into her thoughts. 'Who eventually took you home?'

'I took myself home,' replied Cassandra flatly. 'And Liz was only thinking of me. She—she doesn't trust you.'

'Do you?' The dark eyes gleamed with some emotion Cassandra could not identify, and she found it hard to look away.

'Should I?'

'That depends.' His lips twisted. 'I want you, but you know that. And Liz was right, I was annoyed last night—bloody annoyed. Why did you chicken out on me?'

'I didn't—chicken out.'

'So why didn't you come with me?'

Cassandra shook her head. 'I don't know.'

'Well, at least that's honest,' he remarked dryly. 'Shall I tell you what I think?'

Cassandra shrugged. 'Could I stop you?'

'Yes.'

She made a helpless gesture. 'Go on.'

'Okay.' He paused. 'When I met you at Damon Stafford's reception, you let Liz Lester's comments colour your opinion of me. Oh, I'm not denying she's had grist to her mill. I guess we've all done things we'd rather forget, and I'm no different. But you mustn't believe everything you hear.'

'Nevertheless, you did believe I was married at that time.'

'Sure, I did.' He didn't deny it. 'As I told you last night, I'm no angel. But all you had to do was tell me no and I'd have got the message.'

Cassandra pressed her lips together for a moment. 'So?'

'So, you didn't tell me no, and I discovered that married or not, I needed to know more about *Mrs* Roland.'

Cassandra quivered. 'Needed?'

'Yes, *needed*.' He grimaced. 'I was even prepared to believe that you had an unhappy marriage.'

Cassandra lifted her shoulders. 'How gallant!'

'Yes, wasn't I?' His mouth took on a wry expression. 'Anyway, after that lunch we had together, I made it my business to find out about you and your—late—husband. Mike Roland.' His eyes slanted. 'I'd never have believed it.'

Cassandra frowned. 'Did you know Mike?'

'Personally, no. Of him—of course.' Jay pushed the remainder of his smoked salmon aside. 'Did you love him?'

Cassandra's face gained colour. 'I beg your pardon?'

Jay sighed. 'I'm sorry. If it's painful for you to discuss it, then I won't ask. But from what I hear, he wasn't the most faithful of husbands.'

Cassandra's teeth bit into her lower lip. 'You have no right——'

'I know, I know.' Jay shifted impatiently. 'But, God, Cass, this can't be news to you. Mike Roland used to boast about his conquests. At one time, you couldn't open the sports pages of any newspaper without seeing his face and that of some girl plastered all over it.'

'As you said, you shouldn't believe everything you read in the newspapers,' said Cassandra tightly, then gulped when his hand covered one of hers.

'Okay,' he said, 'I won't say anything else. But you don't have to be afraid of me. I'm not like Mike Roland.'

'Aren't you?' Cassandra met his gaze steadily.

'No,' he assured her flatly. 'Believe me.'

She wanted to. With the warmth of his fingers enclosing hers, his thumb intimately probing her palm, she felt again that stirring sense of excitement. But then the waiter arrived to remove their plates, and embarrassment caused an instinctive withdrawal.

The meal was as good as lunch had been, and endeavouring to lighten the mood, Cassandra brought up the subject of his name. 'Jay,' she said, repeating it cautiously. 'Is that a name or an initial?'

'It's short for James, actually,' he told her without enthusiasm. 'But you can call me Alexei, if you'd rather. Personally, I don't like either of them.'

'Alexei?' Cassandra's eyes widened. 'Of course—that's Russian, isn't it? I suppose your mother chose it.'

'My mother?' Jay's expression grew quizzical, and too late she realised what she had admitted. 'I suppose Liz is responsible for supplying all the dubious facts about my ancestry. I should have known she'd leave no stone unturned.'

'It was Thea, actually,' confessed Cassandra apologetically. 'My mother-in-law. She—well, she remembered when your mother married Sir Giles Fielding.'

'I see.' Jay lay back in his chair. 'And what else did she tell you?'

Cassandra hesitated. 'That—that your grandparents were emigrés at the time of the Revolution.' She sighed. 'I'm sorry if you think I was prying. But—but Thea thought I might find it interesting.'

'And did you?'

Cassandra sighed. 'Yes.'

'I suppose my being a bastard in fact as well as character confirmed the low opinion you had of me?'

'No!' Cassandra caught her breath. 'That's nothing to do with you.'

'It doesn't trouble you, then?'

'Why should it?'

He shrugged, as if reluctantly conceding the point. Then he said: 'Alexei was my grandfather's name, actually. Alexei Ravekov, late of the Tsar's Imperial Guard.' He grinned reminiscently. 'He was quite a fire-eater, the old man.'

Cassandra was intrigued. 'Is he dead now?' she ventured, and Jay's mouth compressed before he nodded.

'He died when I was about twelve years old,' he replied heavily. 'I guess you could say he was the only father I've ever known.'

Cassandra waited until the waiter had served their steaks, and then she said quietly: 'You didn't—regard your stepfather——'

'I was eighteen by the time my mother married Giles,' he told her flatly. 'I left school and went straight to university. I guess you could say we tolerate one another. Nothing more.'

'And—and your grandmother?' The question spilled

from Cassandra's lips before she could prevent it.

'She died before my grandfather,' Jay answered, without hesitation. 'They were very close. I don't think the old man wanted to go on living after Sonya died.'

'Sonya.' The names were so attractive, and yet so alien. 'That was her name.'

'Sofia,' Jay corrected quietly. 'Sonya was the family's name for her. I don't think she ever quite got over having to leave Russia. They lost everything, you see. When they came to England, my grandfather only had enough money to pay their passage. They both had to work to support my mother.'

Cassandra nodded. 'She can't have been very old.'

'No. She was only a baby when they left St Petersburg in 1919.'

It was a fascinating history, and Cassandra would have liked to ask more about his mother, but discretion forebade her. After all, Jay had not mentioned his real father at all, and unless he did, she could not.

When the meal was over and they were leaving the restaurant, Jay suggested a walk. 'Come on,' he said. 'It will do us both good. We can't talk in this place—not unless we go to your room.'

'Or yours,' put in Cassandra swiftly, and his dark brows lifted.

'Well?'

'We'll go for a walk,' she declared tautly, making for the stairs. 'I'll get my coat.'

Jay watched her mount the stairs, and Cassandra was glad they were old and turned back upon themselves at the first landing. She was intensely conscious of his eyes upon her, but she couldn't deny the feeling of excitement just being with him engendered.

In her room, she threw off the jersey dress and replaced it with the trouser suit she had worn to travel in. Tucking the trouser legs into her boots, she surveyed her appearance critically, and then gave an impatient grimace at the flushed expectancy of her features. She must get a hold of herself, she chided, aware that this new confidence was still raw and vulnerable. She had to remember that their relationship was based on a physical attraction, nothing more, and that whatever Jay said, he meant no binding commitment. He was not promising anything, and if she went into this at all, she had to do so with her eyes open, not closed.

Shaking her head, she turned away from the mirror and pulled on the hooded sheepskin she had worn earlier. With its fleecy lining creating a soft frame for her pink cheeks, she was unaware of how delightful she looked, but the man who watched her descending the stairs again had no doubts as to her desirability.

He, too, had put on boots and a fur-lined overcoat, and Cassandra's eyes widened in acknowledgement. 'You went to your room, too?' she murmured, unconsciously seeking his confirmation, and Jay nodded wryly before holding out his hand.

'I went to my room, too,' he agreed, starting towards the porch. 'Come on. It's not snowing at the moment. I'll show you where I used to live.'

Cassandra's surprise at the news that he had once lived in Cambridge was overridden by the disturbing warmth of his hand enclosing hers. She had not yet put on her gloves and nor had he, and with her permission, he drew her hand inside his pocket, warm against the muscled hardness of his hip.

There were few people about in the freezing conditions, but occasionally they encountered groups of students plodding along through the snow. Some of them were even having a snowball fight on the bridge, and Jay grinned goodhumouredly as a fast-moving missile narrowly missed his ear.

'Were you at college here?' Cassandra asked, feeling deliciously warm in spite of the cold air, but Jay shook his head.

'No. I attended university in London,' he told her easily. 'But I worked for a time on the *Cambridge Courier*, and I lived in a room in Pensbury Street.'

'I see,' Cassandra nodded. 'Did you live here long?'

'About fifteen months,' he responded, pausing on the bridge to look down into the icy waters. 'Then I joined the *Post*, and moved back to London.'

'Liz——' Cassandra hesitated, 'Liz said you were a foreign correspondent.'

'That's right, I was.'

'Was?'

'I've been offered a job in television,' he explained carelessly. 'I've been considering whether to take it.'

'In television?' She was impressed.

'I guess I've got tired of travelling,' he declared, turning to rest his back against the stonework of the bridge. 'Living out of suitcases can begin to pall. Maybe I'm getting too old.'

Cassandra's tongue appeared in unknowing provocation. 'You're not old.'

'I'm thirty-four. Considerably older than you.'

'I'm almost twenty-five,' replied Cassandra at once. 'Remember, I've been married.'

'I don't forget,' he told her flatly, and they moved on.

It was after ten when they got back to the hotel, and although they had talked of mostly impersonal subjects, Cassandra felt she knew quite a lot more about him. He had pointed out the room at the top of the old house in Pensbury Street where he used to live, and he had regaled her a little with the stories he had had to cover. He had an amusing turn of phrase, and Cassandra couldn't remember when she had enjoyed herself so much.

'Let's have a drink before we go to bed,' he suggested, as she unbuttoned her coat in the entrance, and she nodded agreeably before preceding him through to the bar.

Like the rest of the public rooms in the hotel, the bar

also had an open fireplace, where smouldering logs were crackling cheerfully. There was a long, crescent-shaped counter, set about with tall stools, and plenty of comfortable armchairs beside square wooden tables. There was music, too, but of a kind that did not intrude upon the guests, and the atmosphere was friendly, warm, and comfortable.

'Let's sit at the bar,' Cassandra suggested, realising as she said so that she was unconsciously avoiding a closer intimacy. If Jay noticed, however, he didn't say anything, and they perched on adjoining stools and ordered their drinks.

'This is nice,' said Cassandra later, sipping the wine she had chosen. 'I've really enjoyed myself this evening.'

'I'm glad.' Jay regarded her between his thick lashes. 'So have I.'

'Have you?' she pressed her lips together. 'Even though this trip was practically forced on you? I know what you said earlier, but—well, I know Thea, and I know what she would say.'

Jay shrugged. 'I would have come anyway.'

Cassandra's eyes widened. 'Why?'

Jay sighed. 'I thought we'd gone into all that.'

'Well——' she chose her words with care. 'I—I hope you won't consider it's been a—a wasted journey.'

'What's that supposed to mean?'

Cassandra glanced nervously about her, half afraid their conversation could be overheard, but there was no one near enough to listen. 'I just mean—I don't intend to—to go to bed with you.'

There was silence for so long that she thought for a moment he was so angry he couldn't speak. But when he did, it was with evident amusement, which upset her more.

'You don't pull your punches, do you?' he remarked, swallowing the remainder of the Scotch in his glass. 'Who taught you to be so candid? I can't believe it was your late husband.'

Cassandra's face burned. 'I just—didn't want you to think——'

'— that you were easy?'

'No.' She felt even more embarrassed. 'Jay, stop teasing me! You know what I mean. You—you were frank with me, so——'

'— so you thought you'd be frank too.'

'Yes.'

'And do you think it's that simple?'

'What do you mean?'

Jay took one of her hands between both of his and separated the fingers. 'I mean do you really think that if I was determined enough to get you into bed, I couldn't do it?'

Cassandra gulped and pulled her hand away. 'Don't do that!'

He shrugged. 'Okay. Let's go to bed.'

She drew a deep breath. 'Yes, let's.'

She was halfway along the corridor to her room when she realised he was following her. She had expected him to follow her upstairs; all the guestrooms were on the first and second floors of the hotel. But now she turned to him anxiously, her confusion evident in her face.

'Where—where are you going?'

'To my room,' he informed her straight-faced. 'You have no objections, do you?'

'Your room is along here?' Cassandra endeavoured to sound casual.

'I'll show you,' he said, overtaking her and pulling out a key from his pocket.

For one awful moment she thought he had a key to her room, but just as indignation rose into her throat, she realised he was opening the door next to hers. The doors were set in pairs, and his was the one beside her own.

'Where else would the manager accommodate husband and wife than next door to one another?' Jay enquired softly, and Cassandra's sigh was rueful as she took the steps that separated them.

'Goodnight, then,' he said, and she nodded rather dully.

'Goodnight,' she answered, pulling out her own key, and by the time she had opened her door, his had closed.

Her room looked less inviting now, and as she tossed her bag on to the bed and removed her coat, she knew a hopeless sense of frustration. The evening had been delightful, but the finale had been a fiasco, and she kicked off her boots impatiently as she spurned her prudish stupidity. It wasn't as if she was a virgin, she thought, grinding her teeth together. What had she to lose, after all? She was letting the things Liz had said and some ridiculous fear she had—and which she didn't understand—prevent her from behaving like the liberated woman she was supposed to be.

Liberated! Her lips curled in distaste. She was not liberated. She was still the same overly-sensitive girl who had married Mike Roland with such high hopes for the future. God, she had been naïve, she thought with disgust. But she had quickly learned. Life was at best a compromise; at worst, it could be a living hell.

She had discovered Mike's inadequacies on their honeymoon. He had taken her to the South of France, and all her friends had envied her his youth and success. Mike had been an idol, a golden boy, a handsome heart-throb, with everything—or so they had believed.

Cassandra supposed she had believed it, too. She had been feted, flattered, made to feel she was someone special. What girl of eighteen wouldn't have responded to that kind of undiluted adulation? No one had expected her to refuse his offer of marriage, and she didn't. She had given up her studies willingly, thrown everything aside for the thrill of becoming Mrs Mike

Roland, a thrill which had lasted just as long as it took them to reach the hotel in St Tropez.

She had sometimes wondered if Mike had ever made it with anyone, but she had never voiced her suspicions. So many girls had flocked around him making a mockery of her theory, and she had believed him when he said she was to blame. Even so, when the idea of divorce had occurred to her, Mike had refused to consider it. Indeed, he became most violent, most abusive, when she suggested leaving him, and she had been too weak—too cowardly, she denigrated herself now—to strike out on her own.

She sat down before the vanity unit and examined her drawn features without pleasure. She looked pale now that memory had robbed her cheeks of their warm colour. Resting her elbows on the shelf of the unit, she cupped her chin in her hands and gazed into eyes made shadowy by her thoughts. What was she doing here? she asked herself silently. Why wasn't she next door, letting Jay Ravek make love to her? That was what she really wanted, wasn't it? Proof that she was not the ice maiden Mike had always declared her to be.

Getting up from the stool, she moved to the windows, drawing the curtain aside and looking out. It was a winter fairyland, a glittering ice-world, in which she was playing the leading role. How much longer was she going to fool herself? She wanted Jay Ravek, just as much as he had said he wanted her. But what could she do about it, when he was next door and she was here?

Her nightgown was lying across the bed, a pretty thing of pale green chiffon, with a matching negligee which she had left at home. She grimaced. She had decided her warm navy candlewick was much more suitable for drifting about the landing at David and Val's, and her lips took on an ironic slant at the sight of its plain serviceability. Hardly the stuff of which *femmes fatales* were made, she reflected ruefully, and thrusting such thoughts aside she went to wash and clean her teeth.

She had rescued her book and was climbing into bed when there was a knock at her door. Immediately, her skin prickled, and the realisation that it could only be Jay beyond the panels filled her with sudden panic. He had come. She was being given a second chance. So why was she sitting here as if Armageddon had been announced?

The knock came again, and this time it was accompanied by a soft voice saying: 'Mrs Roland? I'm sorry to disturb you ...'

The voice was definitely female, and Cassandra's blood subsided. Without stopping to put on her dressing gown, she went hastily to the door, concealing herself behind it as she released the catch.

The woman waiting outside was evidently the housekeeper, and her homely face broke into an apologetic smile. 'I'm so sorry to trouble you and your husband, Mrs Roland, but the manager asked me to tell you that there's been a little breakdown in the plumbing system. The cold weather, you know.' She gave a nervous little laugh. 'He wonders if you'd mind not running any baths first thing in the morning. Until we've had a chance to have it fixed.'

'Of course,' Cassandra smiled. 'We're not used to such cold weather, are we?'

'Well, not such extremes,' agreed the housekeeper, sighing. 'Well, thank you for your trouble, and good-night.'

It was not until Cassandra had closed the door again that she realised the housekeeper had mentioned *Mr* Roland. You and your husband, she had said. But why? Surely they knew they had separate rooms.

As Cassandra considered this disturbing development, her eyes wandered round the room, and almost incredulously they alighted on a door which hitherto she had scarcely noticed. It was in the wall between the two rooms, and because she had not had reason to question its use, she had not paid it any heed. But now it occurred to her that the housekeeper probably thought this linking door was open, and that although she and Jay had separate bedrooms, they did communicate.

Sighing, she caught her lower lip between her teeth. It was obvious she was going to have to let Jay know about the water supply. Heavens, he might even be running a bath at this minute, and that thought sent her across the room to the door to try the handle. Amazingly, it was unlocked, and holding her breath she opened it, only to find a second door beyond. Licking her dry lips, she tried the second door. It was unlocked, too, and her heart palpitated wildly as she turned the handle.

The knocking at her own door was like the thunderous beating of her heart, and she let go of the handle of Jay's door as if it had scalded her. Now what? she wondered, turning back into her bedroom, and almost without thinking she crossed the room to answer it.

'Jay!'

Her shock at finding him outside was mitigated somewhat by confusion. She had been about to enter his bedroom, but now here he was, not only at her door but still fully dressed, apart from his tie and jacket.

'I——' He, too, seemed somewhat bemused at the sight of her, and belatedly she remembered her state of undress. It seemed he was fated to catch her at the most unexpected moments, and shaking her head helplessly, she stepped behind the door.

'What do you want?' she exclaimed, forgetting for a moment that she had been on her way to his room, and with a sigh of impatience he said: 'Do you usually open the door in that condition without asking who's outside?'

'I thought you were the housekeeper,' retorted Cassandra, shivering a little now. 'I—did you know the doors between our two rooms are unlocked?'

'I did know, as a matter of fact,' he agreed, his mouth thinning slightly. 'Look, all I came for was to tell you not to take a bath. They're having some problem with the plumbing.'

Cassandra gasped. 'You know?'

Jay frowned. 'You do, too?'

'How do you think I discovered the doors were open?' she asked a little huskily. Then; 'Aren't you going to bed?'

Jay glanced down at his shirt and trousers. 'Eventually,' he agreed, his eyes guarded. 'Right now, I'm not tired.'

Cassandra quivered. 'Nor am I.'

Jay regarded her for a long moment, then he said quietly: 'Invite me in.'

Cassandra caught her breath. 'Do you want to come in?'

For an answer, Jay stepped between the narrow opening and closed the door behind him. Then, as she wrapped her arms half protectively about herself, he said: 'Did you really think I could sleep, knowing you were in the next room?'

Cassandra's breath escaped unsteadily. 'I can't offer you a drink, because—because I don't have anything.'

'I'm not thirsty,' he assured her tautly.

'I—I wonder if it's started snowing again,' she ventured, hesitating only a moment before gliding across the room to the window to draw a corner of the curtain aside. 'I—no. No, it hasn't.'

She heard him cross the room behind her. She was sensitised to his every movement. But when his hands closed on her hips and drew her back against him, she trembled like a leaf.

Beneath the gauzy folds of her nightgown, her skin gleamed like satin, her flesh soft and creamy, and utterly desirable. Jay would not have been human if he had not groaned a little as the roundness of her thighs yielded against his taut hips, and his hands slid around her to press her even closer.

'Cass——' he breathed, his mouth warm against the side of her neck, and all the pent-up emotions she had been suppressing escaped on a shuddering sigh. Tilting her head back, she let her whole body rest against him, and his hands slid possessively across her flat stomach.

His breath fanned her shoulder, the unsteady intake of his breathing unmistakable proof of the effect just holding her was having on him. Yet he seemed content to hold her like this, allowing her to feel his physical response to her nearness, and she knew a tremulous sense of anticipation in knowing she had this power over him.

As if savouring every moment, his hands moved leisurely over her waist to her ribcage, and from there to the burgeoning fullness of her breasts. She could feel them, hard and swollen, their sharp peaks surging against his palm. Her body seemed poised on the brink of some unknown fulfilment, and although she had no real belief that she was capable of feeling more than this, that inner craving was back, begging assuagement.

Jay's hands grew harder, more possessive, and as if unable to delay any longer, he twisted her round in his arms and looked down at her. His eyes were dark and smouldering, his mouth undeniably sensual, and there was satisfaction in his gaze when he saw the bemused expression on her face.

'We don't need this,' he murmured huskily, sliding the straps of her nightgown from her shoulders, and it fell in a pool on the floor as he swung her off her feet. 'Let's go to bed,' he added, bending his head to cover her mouth with his.

The hotel sheets felt cold at her back, and lying there, waiting while Jay removed his clothes, she knew a returning sense of panic. Dear God, she thought, he was so big, so powerfully masculine. Her experiences with Mike had not prepared her for this.

But when he came down beside her, and his warm body was close to hers, she felt her doubts dissolving again. The searching touch of his lips started a flame inside her, and instead of forcing himself upon her as Mike had used to do, he began to caress her, his hands seeking and finding the most intimate places of her body. At first she objected, her lips moving under his, voicing the protests her puritan upbringing led her to believe was right; but as his mouth continued to possess her, his kisses deepening and lengthening and robbing her of all resistance, she felt herself relaxing, allowing him to do with her as he willed.

She could feel his skin against hers, the hair on his body that arrowed down to his navel and beyond that was so deliciously abrasive to her soft flesh. She could feel his strength and his hardness, and she arched against him eagerly, inviting that ultimate invasion.

'Ah, Cass——' he said unsteadily, and the sudden shifting of his body caused a cool draught of air to touch her skin.

'Don't go,' she begged, her hands at his nape, gripping the hair she found there, and his lips twisted sensually as he gave her reassurance.

'I'm not going anywhere,' he said, his voice thick with emotion, and she shivered ecstatically when his teeth closed over one ripe nipple.

'Jay——' she breathed, half in protest, but she didn't try to stop him, and his mouth moved lower, over her midriff to circle the tender skin of her navel.

'Jay,' she choked, when his mouth slid even lower, but the aching sensation he evoked sent the blood pulsing through her veins.

'You're beautiful,' he murmured, against her trembling flesh. 'Beautiful—and unawakened.' He moved over her. 'Your skin tastes like honey, and I want to taste every inch of you——'

By the time his mouth returned to hers, Cassandra

had lost all sense of time and place. The awareness of her surroundings, the revealing light of the lamp beside the bed, even her own inhibitions, had all given way to a desire to please Jay as he was pleasing her, and her hands began their own investigation. Her fingers slid over the taut skin of his back, discovering the taut bones of his spine, curving over the contours of his hips, finding the experience totally satisfying. She wanted to go on, she wanted to take as long as he had in completing her arousal, but Jay's hands prevented her as she would have continued.

'No, Cass,' he groaned, burying his face against her neck. 'I want you now. I can't wait any longer.'

Cassandra shifted uneasily then. With unwelcome coherence his words had reminded her of all those wasted months and years with Mike, when she had had nothing to sustain her belief in herself except the faint hope that he might be wrong about her. Suddenly, that frail hope didn't seem to be enough. If she was wrong, she would rather not know, and she twisted her head from side to side in an agony of self-recrimination.

'Cass!' Jay's voice was half impatient as she raised her arm to cover her eyes. 'Cass, what's the matter? Don't turn away from me. For God's sake, not now.'

'I—I——' Cassandra's eyes were wild and tearful. 'I can't do this. You don't know about me. I—I'm not like other women——'

Jay's blue eyes narrowed. 'Is that what Roland told you?'

'Yes—no. I mean, I know it's the truth——'

Jay swore softly, but succinctly. 'Oh, Cass, you're crazy,' he breathed, caressing the corner of her mouth with his. 'Doesn't your body tell you you're wrong? I don't know what Roland told you, but believe me, you're everything and more than any man could ever want.'

'I am?' Cassandra still couldn't believe it, but Jay was making her believe it, forcing her to an awareness of her own body's desires, carrying her with him beyond the point of no return.

'God—Cass!' he muttered, as her sweetness enveloped him, and she knew a momentary confusion as the pain she had expected did not materialise. On the contrary, it was a most satisfying experience, and her tenseness fled as he began to move within her. 'Don't—be afraid,' he said roughly, against her lips, and a moist weakness flooded her being . . .

CHAPTER SIX

TIME spiralled back to reality some time around dawn. Cassandra awakened to the awareness of a heavy weight across her breasts, and a warm body close to hers beneath the fluffy quilt. For a moment she was disorientated, shocked into the belief that it was Mike beside her, that Mike was still alive. But even as a wave of horror swept over her at the memory of her husband's violence, Jay stirred, and she turned her head and saw him.

He was still asleep, and in the reflective light from the snow outside, his features had an unexpected vulnerability. With his hair tousled and the darkening shadow of his beard on his jawline, he looked younger and even more attractive, and her limbs weakened instinctively at the remembrance of his lovemaking.

But as her heart somersaulted with sudden emotion, an equally strong sense of panic gripped her. Dear God, she thought unsteadily, she mustn't allow herself to fall in love with him. She knew even now he could hurt her so much more than Mike had ever done.

Yet she could not deny the feelings he had aroused the night before. She had lived for more than twenty-four years believing she was incapable of feeling or inspiring any strong emotion, but now she knew there had never been anything wrong with her. She was neither cold nor frigid. Jay had proved that to her, not once but twice, and in the aftermath of her fulfilment she had confessed the truth to him.

In the morning light, however, she was experiencing an uneasy awareness of how dangerous it might be to give in to those human weaknesses. Jay had given her

90

more than an awareness of her own sensuality. Her admittedly inexperienced desire to find someone—some man—she could have a relationship with bore no relation to what had happened between her and Jay. She had been looking for friendship, companionship, and perhaps love, though again her estimation of the man-woman relationship had been false. What she had found with Jay was more, so much more then she either expected or *wanted*, because she was very much afraid that with him, she could stand no half measures.

After all, he was right. She had been attracted to him at the Stafford reception, but she had not known then how all-consuming that attraction might become. And he was not the kind of man she should—or could—expect any commitment from. Whatever exaggerations Liz had concocted, there was a grain of truth in what she had said, and Jay himself had admitted there had been other women. How many women, Cassandra did not wish to contemplate, acknowledging with a sense of disgust that to picture him in bed with another woman was to imagine the most refined form of torture.

Besides, she told herself severely, she didn't want that kind of commitment either. She had her career to think about, the career she had once before abandoned so cavalierly and lived to regret. One thing seemed certain: she should not ever see Jay again, in case her own weaknesses became evident to him.

She edged reluctantly to the side of the bed, and holding her breath when he shifted in protest, she crawled out on to the floor. Moving quickly about the room, breathing shallowly all the time it took to gather her belongings together, she pushed them into her suitcase. She didn't use the bathroom. She simply collected her toilet bag and toothbrush, and promised herself a shower as soon as she got home.

It was cowardly, walking out on him like this, but she refused to consider any alternative. Yet, when she was dressed, she spent a few moments looking down at his sleeping form, fighting the almost irresistible urge to touch him. Would he understand what she was doing? Would he forgive her? Or would it not occur to him to think that she had to get away before his disturbing personality overrode all practical necessities?

She had to hold on to her own identity. It was no use escaping a disastrous marriage to plunge into a disastrous love affair. Jay might want her now, but how long would it last? Six months? A year, if she was lucky? She couldn't take that—not from him. She knew it. If she was ever foolish enough to put her heart into his keeping, she might never recover again.

There was no one at the reception desk when she went downstairs, but as the rules of the hotel necessitated overnight guests paying for the rooms at the time of booking, she did not feel guilty as she carried her case out to the car.

She did cast a fleeting glance up at the windows of the hotel before pulling through the arch that led out of the parking area, however. She wondered if Jay was still asleep. She hoped so. She had seen the sleek Ferrari parked in its bay and knew better than to imagine the Alfa could hope to outpace it. Her only advantage was the weather. In these conditions, all vehicles were reduced to a similar speed.

The doorbell rang as Cassandra was stepping out of the shower. For a moment she was tempted to pretend she wasn't at home, but then, forcing herself to reason logically, she realised she was only delaying the inevitable. Sooner or later she would have to meet Jay again, and the sooner it was over the better.

Pausing long enough to put on a warm towelling bathrobe, she ran her fingers through the short waves and determinedly walked to the door. She would have preferred to meet him fully dressed, but after last night it would be foolish to exhibit a spurious modesty. Far better to behave as if she had been expecting him. It was the only way she might gain any advantage.

She swung open the door, her expression carefully composed, polite words of greeting on her tongue—and found her mother-in-law outside. Thea was evidently dressed to go out, and she viewed her daughter-in-law's appearance with obvious relief, and without waiting for an invitation stepped past her into the flat.

'You could have rung me,' she began, as Cassandra weakly closed the door behind her. 'I had no idea that you were back until I saw your car downstairs. For heaven's sake, Cass, you knew I would be worried.'

'I'm sorry.' Cassandra spread her hands apologetically. 'I was going to ring you, but I didn't have time for a shower this morning, and I thought——'

'A shower? At two o'clock in the afternoon?' Thea pulled the collar of her fur coat closer about her throat. 'You're sure you're not angry with me? You don't blame me for sending him after you?'

'Blame you?' Cassandra controlled her colour with difficulty. 'Oh, you mean—Jay Ravek——'

Thea sighed. 'Yes, I mean Jay Ravek, and——' she held up her hand as Cassandra would have spoken: 'I should tell you, I rang the King's Arms this morning, and they put me through to your room. It was ten o'clock, and—and he answered.'

'Oh!' Cassandra's cheeks flamed then, and Thea hurried into her explanations:

'I wanted to know what time you were coming back, what time to expect you. The weather has been so bad, and—oh, you know what a worrier I am.'

'It's all right, Thea.'

'It's not all right. I shouldn't have poked my nose in.' Thea sighed. 'Oh, darling, I didn't know what to do when he answered. I'm afraid I just rang off.'

'I see.' Cassandra's lips twisted. Jay must have

wondered who was calling her at that hour of the morning. But one thing was apparent. He had certainly not hurried after her. She had left at seven!

'Did you guess it was me?' Thea looked absurdly anxious, and Cassandra had to comfort her, even though it meant explaining she had not been there.

'I—I left as soon as it was light,' she said, trying to sound casual. 'It seemed the simplest thing to do in the circumstances. I—we—it was a mistake. I—I shan't be seeing him again.'

'Oh, Cass!' Thea looked troubled. 'I feel so responsible.'

'Why?' Cassandra shook her head. 'You didn't make me go to bed with him.'

'I told him where you were. I let him come after you.'

'I don't think you could have stopped him,' retorted Cassandra flatly. 'Jay Ravek is a law unto himself. Don't be silly, Thea. I knew what I was doing.'

'Did you?' Thea studied her pale features apprehensively. 'I suspect you're still an innocent, in spite of everything.' She sighed. 'I only wanted you to see him. To speak to him. I thought—oh, I don't know—he seemed so sincere.'

'He is sincere—in his own way.' Cassandra flopped down on to the sofa and looked up at her mother-in-law, her eyes warm with affection. 'Darling, honestly, he didn't hurt me. He—oh,' she broke off abruptly, digging trembling fingers into her damp hair. 'He was—very kind,' she finished huskily.

Thea glanced at her anxiously, then came down on the couch beside her. 'Cass,' she said earnestly, 'darling, I think we should talk.' She expelled her breath impatiently. 'Damn Peggy Skinner! She made me promise to come over this afternoon. She has this house guest, from South America, who's going to show us some slides of the Indians he's been working with in the Amazon basin. You know what Peggy's like—she always en-

courages these people, and then she has to canvass all
her friends to support them. I told her I really didn't
feel like socialising, what with you being away, but she
wouldn't listen. She said it would do me good to get out
for a while——'

'And so it will.' Cassandra stifled her own disap-
pointment and turned towards her firmly. 'You go,
Thea. You know you'll enjoy it once you get there. And
I—I have plenty to do.'

'Such as what?' Thea looked doubtful.

'Oh, washing, ironing—I've even got some designs to
finish for a Mrs Vance who wants her living-room doing
over——'

'Cass——'

'Out,' declared Cassandra lightly, getting to her feet,
and her mother-in-law was obliged to get up too. 'I'll
see you later,' she added, accompanying her to the door.
'But don't hurry back on my account. I intend to have
an early night.'

With Thea's departure, however, Cassandra experienced an intense feeling of depression. She told herself it
was hardly surprising, in the circumstances, but she was
forced to acknowledge that the news that Jay had still
been at the hotel several hours after her departure was
something she found hard to swallow. She had been
convinced he would follow her. She had been sure that
once he discovered she was gone, he would come after
her. But to learn that he had still been sleeping almost
three hours after she had left the hotel was vaguely
humiliating. And he certainly hadn't rushed back to
town after Thea had made her call. It was almost three
o'clock now.

She stopped herself there. What on earth was she
thinking about? Why should she imagine Jay would let
her know when he got back to town? Why should he?
He had no reason to do so. And until her mother-in-
law rang her doorbell the idea had not even occurred

to her. After all, she had run out on him. He had had what he wanted, so why shouldn't he let her go? It was all part and parcel of what she had been thinking earlier. So far as Jay was concerned, there was no commitment—on either side.

In spite of her reasoning, however, Cassandra found it hard to get through the next few hours. To silence the taunting voices that continued inside her head, she put on an old pair of jeans and a shabby cotton shirt and set about cleaning the apartment. It wasn't big so it didn't take much time, but she got a great deal of satisfaction in working herself to exhaustion. By the time she had finished, the place was gleaming with polish, and the delicious smell of lavender scented the rooms.

Her phone rang around five, but it was only Chris, checking to see whether she had ordered the fabric for re-upholstering a moth-eaten old chaise-longue they had found in the house at Windsor. Most of the furniture they had found in the house had been too eaten up with woodworm to rescue, but the Victorian sofa had been in a reasonable state of repair, and Cassandra had been attracted by its scrolled legs.

'You okay?' asked Chris perceptively, after she had assured him that the material had been ordered. 'You sound down in the dumps. I gather your weekend didn't come off.'

'Something like that.'

Cassandra was non-communicative, and Chris gave a knowing grunt. 'I see. Like that, is it?' he commented drily. 'So—how'd you like yours truly to come round and cheer you up, huh? I could always cook supper. I'm quite a dab hand around the kitchen. I have to be here!'

'No, thanks.'

Cassandra was finding it an effort just being civil at the moment and reluctantly Chris got the message. 'Okay,' he said resignedly. 'But don't say I didn't offer!' and he rang off before she could respond.

Replacing her own receiver, Cassandra knew a momentary pang of regret. She could have done with Chris's inconsequent chatter right now. But it wouldn't be fair to use him, and put his marriage in jeopardy. *Marriage!* Her lips twisted bitterly. Definitely an outmoded institution!

When her doorbell rang at nine o'clock, she went to answer it without hesitation. She assumed it was Thea, back from Mrs Skinner's and ready for a cosy confab over the teacups, but once again she was wrong. This time it was Jay who was propped against the wall beside her door, and she was instantly aware of the sight she must look in the disreputable shirt and jeans, her face bare of all make-up and her hair uncombed. Damn, she thought, why had she allowed resentment and depression to blind her to every eventuality? She should have known a man like Ravek would know all the moves in the game.

'Can I come in?' he enquired expressionlessly, looking over her shoulder, as if he half expected her to have company, and Cassandra took a deep breath.

'Why?'

His mouth took on a downward slant. 'Don't ask silly questions, Cass, there's a good girl.' He straightened away from the wall, impaling her with his dark gaze. 'Are you alone?'

'If it's any concern of yours, then yes, I am,' she replied tautly, though she was far from sure of herself. 'I don't know why you've come here, but——'

'Oh, spare me that, at least,' he exclaimed harshly, moving forward so that she had either to face up to him or step aside. 'Come on, you might as well let me in. I'm not going to leave here until we have this out.'

'Have what out?' But Cassandra moved back anyway, knowing herself for a coward as he strolled into her living room.

'You know what I mean.' He turned to face her as

she reluctantly closed the door, and she thought she could smell whisky on his breath. He was by no means drunk, nor anywhere near it, but her palms moistened anxiously as she waited for him to go on.

'Aren't you going to offer me a drink?' he asked, dark brows quirking above his lean brooding face. He was still wearing the navy suede suit he had worn the night before, but the cream silk shirt was different, and she wondered inconsequently if he had been home to change. Home! She had no idea where his home was, nor indeed, she realised bitterly, whether he lived alone.

'I only have sherry,' she said now, moving her shoulders offhandedly, and he nodded.

'Okay, that will have to do,' he acknowledged, ignoring the fact that she hadn't offered him any, and with a feeling of helplessness, she walked into the kitchen.

When she came back, he was examining the Fragonard print she had bought with the proceeds of her first commission, but he turned politely as she came in and took the glass she reluctantly proffered.

'Aren't you joining me?' he asked, as she took care to avoid touching his fingers, and she shook her head tensely, shunning a reply.

'I like your flat,' he remarked, trying the dry sherry and evidently finding it to his taste. 'Small, but elegant.' He paused. 'Like you.'

'I'm not small,' she retorted, nonetheless aware of her low heels. 'I'm five feet six.'

'Minds are not always relevant to physical stature,' he responded mockingly, raising his glass, and Cassandra's breathing quickened in tenor with her pulse.

It was useless to pretend she could dismiss the fact that less than twenty-four hours ago, they had been dining together. Despite her enforced detachment, she couldn't help being aware of him, and her brain could not erase the knowledge of how he had looked without his clothes . . .

'You did expect me to come, didn't you?' he continued, studying the liquid in his glass. 'You didn't really think you could walk out on me this morning, without so much as a gesture of farewell?'

'I—I thought it was the best thing to do,' Cassandra replied quickly.

'Best for whom?' he countered, meeting her eyes.

'Why, for both of us, I suppose.' She linked her fingers together. 'I'm afraid I'm not very experienced in these matters.'

'And I am?' The dark eyes snapped fire.

Cassandra drew an unsteady breath. 'Aren't you?'

Jay finished the sherry and put the glass down on the record cabinet. 'Liz has done a pretty thorough job of character assassination, hasn't she?' he remarked, folding his arms. 'But didn't she also tell you that my—conquests generally last longer than one night?'

Cassandra unlinked her fingers to run one hand uneasily into her hair. 'Oh, look,' she said uncomfortably, 'is all this necessary? I mean, surely it's obvious——'

'What is obvious?'

'Well, my leaving you, of course. Surely you realised what it meant?'

'No.' His face was brooding. 'What did it mean?'

He was not making it easy for her, and Cassandra wished with all her heart that she had prepared herself better for this encounter. 'Last night,' she began carefully, choosing her words, 'last night was a mistake——'

'It was?'

'Yes. It should never have happened. I behaved—very badly. I—I don't know what came over me.'

'*I* came over you,' Jay inserted harshly. 'And it was no mistake. You wanted me, Cass, just as much as I wanted you.'

'Well, perhaps——'

'Stuff it, Cass. There's no perhaps about it. For years you've been nursing the belief that you were to blame for Roland's hang-ups, but last night I showed you——'

'I'd really rather not talk about Mike——'

'Why? Am I scraping a nerve? Goddammit, Cass, that's over now. Roland's dead and you're alive! Or you were last night!'

Cassandra trembled. 'If you want me to thank you——'

'To thank me!' Jay uttered a savage oath. 'For God's sake, Cass, stop talking such utter rubbish! I didn't come here for your thanks. That's a bloody insult!'

Cassandra held up her head. 'Then why did you come? I can't believe last night meant that much to you. You were still in bed at ten o'clock this morning!'

'Oh, I see.' Jay's lips twisted. 'Your mother-in-law has been talking. Did she think I wouldn't recognise her voice if she rang off? You can tell her I've been a journalist too long to be duped that easily.' He shook his head. 'And that mattered to you, did it? That I was still occupying the confessional couch?'

Cassandra was annoyed that she had betrayed herself so obviously, and she hastily tried to retract: 'All I'm saying is that for someone who's supposed to be so interested in why I walked out, you've taken an unconscionably long time to get here!'

Jay inclined his head. 'Point taken. And I'm willing to explain.'

'I don't need your explanations——'

'Nevertheless, you're going to get them,' he retorted flatly. 'To begin with, I was not asleep when you made your furtive departure. You woke me up when you crept out of bed, but I let you believe otherwise because I wanted to see what you planned to do.'

'You—you shouldn't have done that.'

'How so?' He shrugged. 'I didn't want to spoil your fun. And besides, by the time I realised what you intended, it was too late to do anything about it.'

Cassandra clenched her fists. 'You watched me!'

'With interest,' he agreed shortly. 'Then,' he added, deliberately baiting her, 'as I was tired, I went back to sleep.'

Cassandra burned with embarrassment. 'I—I don't see that any of this is—is relevant.'

'Don't you? Well, let me continue.' He exhaled heavily. 'When next I wakened, it was after nine, and my temper hadn't improved with keeping. On the contrary, if you'd been around, I think I'd have wrung your bloody neck, for making a fool of me!'

'I—making a fool of you?' Cassandra was taken aback, but Jay was not finished.

'What else?' he declared harshly. 'We were supposed to be married, you know.' He shook his head. 'I was in no mood to be understanding, as your mother-in-law would have found out if she hadn't let discretion act the better part of valour!'

'Even so——'

'Even so—nothing.' Jay's mouth was hard. 'I drove back to London, torn between the urge to beat your brains out and the equally strong desire to drown all thoughts of you in a malt-based anaesthetic!'

'But you came here.'

'Eventually,' he agreed grimly. 'Because it occurred to me that I might have misjudged you, that I might have misinterpreted the intention behind your untimely decampment.'

Cassandra moved her shoulders. 'I—I'm sorry you've had a wasted journey.'

'What do you mean?' His eyes narrowed.

'I mean—I'm not sorry about leaving you this morning. The mistake was in letting—letting it happen in the first place.'

'You think so?' He looked impatiently at her. 'Cass, you're not making sense.'

'I thought I was.' Cassandra forced herself to continue: 'Last night—happened. I can't alter that. But I can make sure it doesn't happen again.'

Jay stared at her incredulously. 'Why would you want to do that?' He made a helpless gesture. 'Last night was *good*, Cass. We were good together.'

Cassandra's tongue circled her lips. 'I'd rather not have a discussion about it——'

'The hell you wouldn't!' Jay's temper surfaced a little. 'So what are you trying to say? That I should say thanks very much, and walk out of here?'

Her chest felt constricted. 'Is that so surprising?'

Jay breathed noisily. 'You tell me.'

Cassandra bent her head. 'I'm sure you don't need me to tell you the rules of the game, Jay. Let's not pretend last night was the preliminary to a declaration of marriage. We both know that's not true. I—I wouldn't want it to be true,' she hastened quickly, in case he should get the wrong impression. 'It was a—a pleasant experience——'

'A pleasant experience!' Jay's oath was crude. 'For God's sake, Cass, don't give me that. Last night you discovered you were a woman, and I helped you make that discovery. It was no—pleasant experience! It was fantastic, and you know it. Stop kidding yourself. We can't give up something like that.'

'We must.' Cassandra took a backward step, dismayed to discover his words were a powerful intoxicant in themselves. 'Jay, I'm sorry if you thought I—I wanted an affair with you. I—I am grateful to you, but I—I can't get involved in that kind of a relationship——'

Jay watched her intently. 'Why not?'

Cassandra's nerves stretched. 'Oh, I don't know,' she exclaimed distractedly. 'It's not what I want. I—I'm a

career person. I can't afford these kind of distractions.
I—I admit that—that once I did think I was the kind
of person who could have that kind of relationship,
but I'm not! I suppose, having been married——'

'You weren't *married*!' Jay overrode her savagely.
'You only lived with a man!'

'In—in spite of the fact that I was married,' she persisted unevenly, 'I don't want that kind of relationship
now. I'm sorry, but there it is.'

'So what am I supposed to do?'

'You?' Cassandra was confused. 'I—I don't know what
you mean.'

'I mean, if I don't accept this?' His mouth twisted
self-derisively. 'Incredible as it is, I still want you. So
what am I to do about that?'

Cassandra's knees felt like jellies. This was a situation
she had never dreamt of having to handle. If she had
anticipated this scene at all, it was in terms of his contempt and anger, never his forbearance. It disconcerted
her, and unnerved her, not least because she guessed he
could be a formidable adversary . . .

'I think you'd better go,' she said at last, nervously,
steeling herself against his unconscious attraction, and
his hands fell loosely to his sides.

'Okay,' he said, and her initial reaction was one of
intense relief that he was letting her off so lightly. But
his next words had her groping for support. 'We'll get
married,' he said indifferently, almost as if he was discussing the weather. 'So long as you don't expect
church bells and flowers, and some long-winded
parson to give us his blessing! The register office will
do very well, and as long as it's legal, what do you
care?'

Cassandra gasped. She was shocked. His proposal was
so completely improbable. And he evidently expected
her to agree. She found it almost insulting. Something
had to be said. Somehow she had to dismiss his propo-

sal, and quickly, before its attractions got the better of her.

'M—marry you?' she echoed at last, her voice several octaves higher than normal. 'You—must be joking!'

Jay's mouth drew into a tight line. 'No, I am not joking. Nor do I enjoy hearing my perfectly reasonable proposition spoken of in that tone.'

'I see.' Cassandra was a trembling mass of jelly, but she managed to proceed. 'Well, I don't think you should make a mockery of marriage.'

'Don't be so bloody childish! I'm not mocking it.'

'Aren't you?'

Jay took a step towards her. 'Let me show you——'

'No!' She was very definite about that. 'I—I want you to get out of here—*now*!'

To her dismay, there was a tremor in her voice when she spoke, and she prayed he would not realise how precariously her defiance was balanced.

'Cass——' He must have realised it, she thought unsteadily, as his tone took on a sensuousness that sent unwilling shivers of excitement up her spine. If he touched her now, she would be lost, she thought fatalistically. She would never be able to send him away, and he would instantly guess the truth.

'Cass——' He said her name again, and her heart almost stopped beating when his hands descended on her shoulders. It was too late now to try to step back from him, and she might precipitate his actions if she tried to drag herself away. 'Cass, why do you go on fighting me?' he demanded, his thumbs stroking the taut lines of her throat. 'We were so good together. Don't you want to see how much better it can be?'

'No!'

But her denial was a plaintive cry that he ignored as he drew her towards him. The warm clean smell of his body enveloped her, the delicious fragrance of his skin lightly imbued with some tangy shaving lotion mingling with his scent of maleness. It wasn't fair, she thought, her cheek brushing the velvet texture of his lapel. Being near to him like this was actual physical torment, and for the first time in her life she ached for a man's possession. But not any man, just this man, she acknowledged despairingly, and gave her lips up to his kiss.

'Ah, Cass——' he groaned, his mouth sending her senses spinning in mindless rapture, and as passion leapt between them, she was helpless to resist. His hands slid proprietorially over her back to her hips, probing beneath her shirt and pressing her to him. She felt the stirring muscles between his legs, and as his possessive fingers brought her firmly against his hardness, the quivering, betraying weakness in the pit of her stomach made her a prisoner in his grasp . . .

The chime of her doorbell was like the voice of reason fighting back the powers of darkness, and Cassandra drew an uncertain breath. 'Thea!' she breathed, pressing her hands against his chest, and with a muffled oath Jay was forced to let her go.

'Get rid of her,' he muttered, raking back his hair with an unsteady hand, revealing he was not as controlled now as he had been earlier, but Cassandra had very definite ideas about who wanted getting rid of.

'Darling!' she exclaimed eagerly, opening the door, and grasping Thea's arm before she could move away. 'Come in, come in! I was beginning to wonder where you'd got to.'

'Oh, you know Peggy Skinn——' Thea was beginning in a vaguely bewildered tone, when she caught sight of Jay, motionless across the room. 'But you've got company, Cass. I—don't want to intrude——'

'Jay was just leaving,' declared Cassandra flatly, ignoring his sudden intake of breath. 'I—I think we've said all there is to say to one another, haven't we?' She didn't give him a chance to reply before adding: 'If ever you need your apartment renovating, however——'

'Cass——'

'Cass——'

They both spoke simultaneously, Thea evidently embarrassed by the invidiousness of her position, Jay's face contorted with an anger he made no attempt to conceal.

'Please——' Cassandra drew an uneven breath and pressed her hands together. 'It—it's late. I wish you would go, Jay. I—I—it's no use. I'm sorry.'

Thea exchanged a troubled look with the man, her expression mirroring her confusion, and as if respecting the older woman's position, Jay pushed his hands into the pockets of his jacket.

'Okay,' he said flatly. 'Okay, I'll go.' He walked across the floor and paused before Cassandra. 'But it's not over, Cass, believe me. I'll be seeing you again.'

'I don't think so,' Cassandra countered tremulously, and with a sound of frustration Jay strode out of the door, allowing it to slam behind him.

CHAPTER SEVEN

THE heat in the sauna was stifling, and Jay could feel the sweat pouring out of him. Great droplets of moisture rolled down his face from the lustreless mat of his hair, and the towel thrown carelessly across his thighs barely soaked up the perspiration running from his chest and shoulders. It was hardly a satisfying experience, more a tortuous endurance before the delightful coolness of the pool, but despite the steamy atmosphere, Jay's mind was crystal clear.

He was going to leave the *Post*, but not, as he had once considered, to accept the job he had been offered by one of the London television companies. He was going to make a complete break with journalism and do what he had planned to do for some years now. He was going to find a place in the country, far enough from town to discourage casual callers, and he was going to try and write the book he was sure he had in him.

It was an appealing idea, and one he had toyed with on and off for the past eighteen months, ever since the life he had been leading had begun to pall. He had enjoyed his work, he *still* found journalism challenging; but he wanted more out of his life than an epitaph that read: *Killed in the pursuit of ambition!*

He had spoken of his plans to his editor the night before. Of course, Hal Ames hadn't wanted him to resign, for either reason, and he had used every trick in the book to try and change his mind. The chances of him writing anything worth publishing were unlikely at best, Hal had said scathingly, but Jay had stuck to his decision with dogged determination.

'What the hell's wrong with you?' Hal had demanded at last. 'Don't tell me some female's got her claws into you at last! God Almighty, Jay, whoever she is, she can't be worth what you're considering giving up!'

'There is no female,' Jay assured him flatly. 'Can you imagine any of the girls I know being prepared to abandon their social life in favour of a cottage in the country?'

'I can think of a few,' retorted Hal drily.

Jay sighed. 'Hal, I'm sick to my teeth with the life I'm leading here. And besides——' he paused, 'right now, it suits me to get out of London.'

Hal sighed. 'Okay, okay. But for how long?'

'How long—what?'

'How long before you get rid of this writing bug?'

Jay lifted his shoulders. 'As long as it takes. Maybe forever.'

'Forever!' Hal was appalled. 'Hell, Jay, you can't mean that!' He shook his head. 'I give it nine months—no,' this as Jay's eyes hardened, '—a year. I'll give you a year to get this—this foolishness out of your system. After that, we talk again, right? I can't say fairer, can I?'

Jay shifted now, getting up from the stone slab where he had been lying, and walking to the door. Outside, the air struck him with a blast of coolness, even though the area around the swimming pool was heated. But after the sweltering humidity of the sauna, anywhere would feel cool, and shedding his towel, he dived smoothly into the water.

It was like silk against his moist skin, rinsing away all impurities, leaving him feeling sharp and alert. With real enjoyment he swam strongly to the end of the pool and back again, prolonging the feeling of well-being, loath to leave the undemanding freedom of the club. This was something he would miss, he reflected. He always took advantage of its superlative facilities when he was in London.

Thirty minutes later, refreshed, dried, and dressed in beige slacks and a tan leather jerkin, he left the health club and drove his green Ferrari across town to his apartment in Winslow Court. It was barely eight o'clock when he let himself into his flat on the eighth floor and his housekeeper, Mrs Temple, was just preparing his breakfast.

Although the apartment boasted a dining room, as well as a spacious living room, Jay invariably ate breakfast in the kitchen, preferring the informality. It gave him an opportunity to speak to Mrs Temple, and she enjoyed telling him the latest news about her son and daughter-in-law who had emigrated to Canada. Mrs Temple had been with Jay for more than ten years, ever since his salary enabled him to lease this apartment and employ a housekeeper, and although he had spent months of every year out of the country, he could always rely on Mrs Temple being there whenever he needed her.

'Good morning,' she greeted him warmly as he came into the kitchen, and Jay lifted his eyes from the newspaper he was scanning to give her a faintly abstracted smile.

' 'Morning,' he responded, subsiding on to a stool at the breakfast bar and looping one leg round its stem. 'It's a cold day, isn't it? I hope we're not going to have any more snow.'

'The daffodils are out in the park,' remarked Mrs Temple, pouring him some coffee. 'I saw them on my way over. Real pretty they looked, too.'

Jay nodded, thanking her for the coffee, and as he put his newspaper aside, Mrs Temple pursed her lips with importance. 'Mr Conway rang,' she announced. 'About fifteen minutes ago. I said I'd ask you to ring him back.'

'Guy?' Jay frowned. 'Did he say what he wanted?'

'No.' Mrs Temple shook her head. 'But I don't suppose it's anything that can't wait until after you've had your breakfast.'

Jay grimaced. 'I doubt he'd agree with you,' he remarked humorously. 'It's not like Guy to be out of bed before nine o'clock. It must be something important, or he wouldn't have made the effort.'

Mrs Temple snorted. 'Well, don't you go letting this meal spoil, or I'll have a few words to say to Mr Conway next time he comes here.'

Jay grinned, and levered himself up from the stool to go and ring his friend and colleague. Guy Conway worked for the commercial television station who had offered Jay a job. They had been friends since their student days, and the fact that Guy was married now had made little difference to their friendship.

'Hi there!' Guy's response to Jay's call was characteristically enthusiastic. 'How are you? You haven't forgotten Helen and I are expecting you for dinner on Friday, have you?'

Jay lounged lazily on to a soft green velvet sofa. 'I'm sure you didn't ring me at eight a.m. just to ask me that,' he countered drily. 'What is it? Can't it wait until Friday?'

'Actually, no.' Guy was serious now. 'I wanted to catch you before you left for Frankfurt. You did say you were going to Frankfurt today, didn't you?'

'This evening,' agreed Jay blandly. 'But you could have caught me at the office.'

'I didn't know what time you were leaving,' Guy explained, 'and ringing your office doesn't always work—you're so seldom in it!'

'Okay, point taken.' Jay lifted one booted foot to brush a speck of lint from the hem of his slacks. 'So what is it that can't wait? Helen's not ill or anything, is she?'

'No, no.' Guy was impatient. 'It's nothing to do with Helen. Only—well, were you really serious the other night when you spoke about finding yourself a house out of town?'

Jay sat up. 'Yes, I was serious. You know that.'

'Okay, okay, don't get uptight about it.' Guy was also perceptive. 'It just so happens we may be able to help you.'

'Indeed?'

'Yes. There's a house in Combe Bassett, that's a village in Oxfordshire, that sounds exactly what you want.'

Jay's interest kindled. 'You've seen an advertisement?'

'No.' Guy hesitated. 'As a matter of fact, it belongs to Helen's aunt and uncle.'

'And they're selling?'

'No, again.'

'Guy——' Jay was growing impatient, but his friend interrupted him.

'Let me tell you. I know you said you wanted to buy somewhere, Jay——'

'I do.'

'—but—well, we don't want to lose touch with you, and if you buy some place miles from anywhere, you're going to find it bloody hard to sell again when the time comes.'

Jay sighed. 'Don't you mean—*if* the time comes?'

'Okay.' Guy acknowledged the point. 'Even so, I think you're crazy if you go ahead and buy a house without finding out whether you can stand that kind of life.'

Jay breathed deeply. 'I guess you have a point.'

'Sure I do.' Guy was eager. 'At least think about it.'

'What about Helen's relations? Where do they come in?'

'They don't.' Guy paused. 'They're retiring, and they plan to pay a prolonged visit to Helen's other aunt in

Australia. They need someone to caretake the house for them. When I told them about you, they were delighted.'

Jay drew a deep breath. 'I've not said I'll take it, Guy.'

'I know that. But promise me you will think about it.'

Jay shrugged his shoulders. 'Okay, I'll think about it.'

'You can let us know your decision on Friday.'

'Fine.' Jay changed the subject. 'How's Helen?'

'Oh, she's okay.' Guy was matter-of-fact. 'How about Mrs Roland? Have you seen her lately?'

'No.'

Jay was abrupt, and his mood of well-being dispersed beneath a sudden wave of irritation. Two months ago, in an alcohol-induced state of melancholy, he had confessed his admiration for Mike Roland's widow, and although he had not told Guy everything, he had regretted it ever since. His abortive attempts to see Cassandra since that night in Cambridge were a source of bitter self-contempt, and although they, too, were several weeks ago now, his pride was still smarting.

'I only wondered,' Guy ventured now, sensing the uncertain ground he was treading, 'because as a matter of fact, I saw her myself last night, at Paul Ludlum's party.'

The muscles in Jay's stomach tautened, and although he knew he was all kinds of a fool, he asked: 'Who's Paul Ludlum?'

'Don't you know him?' Guy was tentative. 'He's an accountant. Mrs Roland's accountant, I gather, although my guess is he'd like to be something more.'

'Really?' Jay found he wanted to end this conversation now, but Guy wasn't quite finished.

'Yes,' he said thoughtfully. 'And I have to agree with you, she is a very attractive lady. Though I did think she looked a little pale. Maybe she's working too hard. Ludlum tells me she has a very successful interior-designing business.'

'I'm really not interested in Mrs Roland's commercial abilities,' Jay remarked, with cutting emphasis. 'I'll think about your proposition while I'm away, Guy, and I'll get back to you.'

'You do that.' Guy was forced to accept his dismissal, and Jay rang off without offering Helen his usual good wishes.

His breakfast was waiting for him, and he gulped down a glass of orange juice before looking at the food on his plate. The sight of grilled bacon and mushrooms, and lightly fried eggs, revolted him suddenly, and ignoring Mrs Temple's speculative gaze, he picked up the newspaper and assumed an interest in its pages.

He hoped Mrs Temple would leave him to get on with it as she often did, going about her work in the flat with her usual attention to detail. He could scrape the contents of his plate into the waste disposal unit in the sink, and she would be none the wiser. But this morning Mrs Temple chose to linger, and eventually tutted at the congealing food.

'What did Mr Conway have to say to make you lose your appetite?' she exclaimed, with the familiarity of long service. 'Goodness me, you haven't touched your meal. I thought you were hungry.'

'I'm sorry, Mrs Temple.' Jay forced a politeness he was far from feeling. 'It must be because I've got other things on my mind. I promise I'll do better tomorrow.'

'You won't be here tomorrow,' retorted Mrs Temple, sighing as she picked up his plate and herself emptied its contents into the sink. 'Have you forgotten? You're off to Frankfurt. And I don't suppose you'll get a proper breakfast there.'

'You'd be surprised.' Jay determinedly cast his black mood aside. 'Anyway, I'm glad you reminded me. Did you pack a dinner suit?'

'I put in your black velvet dinner jacket,' Mrs Temple agreed thoughtfully. 'But you're coming back tomorrow night, aren't you?'

'Late,' said Jay, nodding. 'I have to attend a reception before I leave, and I'll come straight on to the airport. The black jacket is ideal. Thanks.'

Mrs Temple sighed. 'Are you sure you're all right, Mr Ravek? I've thought myself that you've been looking a little tired lately. Are you sleeping properly?'

Jay grimaced. 'Well, I'm sleeping alone,' he remarked, refusing to allow her words to rekindle his frustration. 'Maybe that's what's wrong with me.' His dark eyes danced. 'I must be lonely.'

Mrs Temple chuckled, though her face had turned red with confusion. 'I know you're teasing me, Mr Ravek. You're not short of a young lady to—well, you know what I mean.'

'Do I, Mrs Temple?'

'Away with you, of course you do.' Mrs Temple waved a teasing hand at him, and then left the kitchen to attend to her other duties.

After she had gone, Jay poured himself another cup of coffee, and thought about the house Guy had suggested. It might be a good idea to rent a property. He didn't want to sell this apartment, and keeping two homes going was an added expense. As yet, Mrs Temple knew nothing of his plans, but he was reasonably sure she would be prepared to go with him. She had said several times that since her son had left for Canada she had few ties in London, and as her husband had died before she started working for Jay, she would probably welcome the change.

As to the rest of what Guy had said, Jay refused to let his friend's comments about Cassandra arouse his antagonism. So far as he was concerned, she no longer existed, and any compunction he had felt for the way he had behaved had been savagely dispelled by her contempt for his feelings. He had thought she was different. He had actually believed he had at last found a woman he wanted to share some time with. But he had been proved wrong, and his bitterness towards her was compounded by the suspicion that she had been fooling him all along. He had even begun to doubt the kind of relationship she had had with her husband, and had almost succeeded in convincing him that her innocence had all been just an act.

It was this that irritated him most, this and the unwilling awareness that no matter how he tried, he could not forget the satisfaction he had found with her . . .

It could be said that Jay's health was in an infinitely sweeter state than his temper when he flew into Heathrow late the following evening. He had drunk steadily throughout the two-hour flight, an unusual circumstance for him, and by the time he walked into the arrivals lounge at Terminal 2, he was in no mood to be civil to anyone.

The whole trip had been a waste of time. He had been sent out to Frankfurt to interview Johann Richter, a German politician, whose right-wing tendencies were causing the democratic government some embarrassment, without even gaining a private conversation with the man. Richter had been surrounded by bodyguards every time he left his apartment, and the reception he was supposed to have attended this evening had been cancelled at the last minute. Jay's interview with him had been meant to coincide with his current election campaign, but his advisors had warned him off, and Jay's journey had been for nothing.

The taxi ride into the city gave him plenty of time

to review the reasons for his foul mood, and honesty compelled him to admit that Herr Richter's attitude had not been entirely to blame. All day he had fought off a crippling feeling of depression, engendered by something that had happened the night before: an attractive German girl had attracted his attention in the bar of his hotel. She had been young and blonde and beautiful, and in the normal way Jay would have had no compunction about taking what she was so obviously offering. Instead, he had ignored her invitation, smiled, and said a polite goodnight—simply because she had aroused no sexual urge whatsoever!

It was not a satisfying situation. He had not felt any interest in the opposite sex for more than two months now, and although up until now he had succeeded in convincing himself that he was tired of all the familiar faces, that compromise no longer held true. It didn't make sense, and he didn't know what to do about it.

Guy rang him on Friday morning, ostensibly to remind him he was coming to dinner that evening. 'Did—er—did you give the house some thought?' he asked, revealing his real reason for ringing, and Jay concealed his impatience and said he was prepared to go and look at it.

'I'll give you the details this evening,' Guy exclaimed delightedly, evidently well pleased, and Jay hoped he would not live to regret agreeing so impulsively.

It was a bitterly cold day, and when Jay left his office at four o'clock that afternoon, a biting wind was blowing up the Strand. It was a relief to get inside the Ferrari, cold though it was, and he tried to dispel his dour mood by giving the vehicle its head. One could rely on machinery, he reflected gloomily, pulling ahead of a slow-moving pantechnicon. If one treated machinery correctly, it remained in good working order, and no stupid reflex like emotion could foul up the gears.

He parked the Ferrari in the garage below his apartment and carried his leather folder into the lift. He had brought some work home with him, hoping he could concentrate more easily away from the distracting influences of the press room, but he doubted it. Lord, he wasn't impotent, was he? he asked himself savagely, and then thrust the disquieting thought aside as the lift stopped at his floor.

Mrs Temple had gone home. She knew he was dining out this evening, and Jay tossed his fur-lined parka on to one of a pair of sofas and went to fix himself a drink.

Mrs Temple had left a list of calls that had come in for him on the pad beside the phone, and while he swallowed a double Scotch and soda he scanned the names. His mother had phoned, he noticed wryly, and there had been a call from a fellow correspondent, who had just returned to England after a spell in the Far East. The only other call had apparently been from a woman who had not left her name, and he could only assume it was someone who preferred to keep their association private. Even so, Jay was slightly perplexed. He couldn't think of anyone offhand who might fit into this category, and he cast the pad aside, too restless just now to return anyone's call.

He was engrossed in the file he had prepared on Johann Richter when the doorbell chimed, breaking his mood. Swearing to himself, he got up from the couch and went to answer it. He was only just beginning to get interested in what he was doing, and only the thought that it might be Mrs Temple who had forgotten her key forced him to be sociable. Massaging the muscles at the back of his neck, he jerked open the door, and felt an immediate—and unwanted—stirring in his loins.

'Hello, Jay.'

With a feeling compounded of anger and outright disbelief, he regarded the young woman facing him with raw hostility. What the hell was she doing here? After the way she had hung up on him last time he phoned her, he had felt an intense desire never to set eyes on her again, and now here she was, disrupting what little sanctuary he had left.

'I'm sorry if I'm disturbing you.' She was speaking again, and he forced his mind back from the chasm of his thoughts. 'I—I did ring earlier, but you weren't at home, and I—I thought it might be better if—if I came to see you.'

Jay stared at her grimly, aware for the first time that her face did look thinner than he remembered. What had Guy said—that she looked pale? She didn't look pale now. Her colour was almost hectic. But he suspected it was on account of the apprehension she was feeling in coming uninvited to his apartment. She was still attractive, though, that much he had to concede, her fair hair longer than it had been previously, curling in soft tendrils about her cheeks. She was wearing a dark red cape, that hid her slender figure, but the hood was thrown back and the black fur lining etched her face. It angered him that he still found her appearance captivating, and his voice revealed his anger as he was obliged to make some response.

'What do you want?' he demanded, and there was no trace of compassion in his tone. 'I'm rather tied up just now. I don't have time for—social calls.'

'This isn't a social call.' Cassandra's soft lips drew into a troubled line, and she glanced with obvious emphasis over her shoulder. 'Do—do you think I might come in for a moment? I—well, I have to talk to you.'

Jay made no move to allow her to cross his threshold. On the contrary, he knew an almost paranoic desire to keep her out of his apartment, and his voice was harsh as he repulsed her.

'What's the matter, Mrs Roland?' he taunted. 'Don't tell me you've changed your mind and decided to accept my proposal after all. I'm sorry.' He was derisive. 'It wasn't an open-ended offer. I'm afraid it's been withdrawn.'

He knew he had hurt her by the suddenly pained expression he glimpsed in the long green eyes. Long lashes, silver-tipped like her hair, swept down to hide that knowledge from him, but not soon enough. He saw the bruised hollowing of their depths, and in spite of himself his conscience smote him.

But she was already turning away, groping almost blindly along the corridor towards the lift. The unexpected compunction that made him speak her name went on deaf ears, and he was forced to stride along the corridor after her to bring her to a standstill.

She fought him then, her arm moving uselessly in the effortless grip of his fingers, and his mouth compressed tightly before he gestured back to his door.

'I was rude, and I apologise,' he said grimly, the reluctance of his apology evident even to his ears. 'I suggest you come back and tell me what it is that's so important, and I'll try and remember you're a lady.'

Cassandra caught her breath at his insolence. 'It doesn't matter,' she declared tautly. 'I—I didn't want to come here in the first place. If you'll let go of my arm, I'll go away as you obviously would prefer me to do, and I'll try and forget your ignorance!'

Jay looked down into those determinedly defiant green eyes now, and knew a violent urge to smother her protests with his mouth. She was so stiff, so indignant— and despite everything that had gone before, he couldn't forget how she had made him feel . . .

'You're coming back with me,' he said, his tone brooking no argument. 'Now, do you come willingly, or do I drag you by your hair?'

Cassandra tore herself free of him, brushing down the

skirt of her cape with unknowing provocation. 'As you can threaten me with brute force, what choice do I have?' she demanded, and he acknowledged her unwilling capitulation. They walked back to the apartment in silence, and after urging her into the lamplit living room, Jay closed the door and leaned back against it with apparent indolence. Only he wasn't indolent: anything but. And the discomfiting awareness of his own arousal was by no means reassuring in these circumstances.

Fortunately Cassandra seemed unaware of his problems. Evidently she had problems of her own, and he wondered what sudden catastrophe could have precipitated this foray into the enemy's camp. For she clearly had no heart in what she was doing, and could only have been persuaded by somebody else. Who? Her partner? Her mother-in-law? Liz Lester? His mouth took on a downward slant. He doubted it. Liz Lester would not encourage their relationship.

'Won't you take off your coat?' he enquired now, with forced politeness. 'Can I get you a drink? Some coffee?'

'I don't want anything.' Cassandra stood in the centre of the huge Persian carpet, looking about her as if she hoped she might find some safe bolthole into which to crawl. Her fingers moved to the frogged fastening of her cape almost convulsively, and then took several nerve-racking moments to release the toggles. She concentrated on the task with apparently total absorption, and Jay's own nerves tightened as the minutes stretched. But at last the cape was free, and she slipped it off her shoulders, allowing it to fall gracefully on to the couch beside his parka.

Earlier, he had drawn the heavy velvet curtains across the long windows, and now they formed a dark backcloth to her pale beauty. She was wearing a cream suede dress, fringed at the hem and loosely knotted at the waist with a leather thong. Brown suede boots hid the remainder of her legs, but his eyes were drawn to the stark pallor of her features. She had never looked so frail before, but equally, she had never looked more vulnerable.

'Sit down.' He straightened away from the door, his voice curt and insensitive, an unconscious effort to destroy the effect she was having on him, and she shook her head in vigorous negation.

'I—I prefer to stand,' she said tautly, and with an indifferent shrug Jay strolled across the carpet.

He was badly in need of a drink, he realised irritably, and it took an effort not to let the bottle of Scotch clatter against his glass. 'Well?' he said, after swallowing half what he had poured. 'Won't you come to the point? I assume there is a point, or you wouldn't be here.'

'You're so right.' Cassandra spoke vehemently, unknowingly fuelling his resentment. Then, almost as if she was playing for time, she added: 'This is a beautiful apartment.'

'I like it.' Jay spoke carelessly. 'The fruits of a misspent youth, you might say.'

'Did you misspend your youth?' Cassandra turned to him in unexpected enquiry, and Jay's patience snapped.

'For God's sake, Cass,' he grated, 'you didn't come here to ask about my youth. What do you want? Who has forced you to come here, when you would so obviously rather be elsewhere?'

Cassandra pressed her palms together in an unconscious gesture of supplication. 'Is it so obvious?'

'To me—yes.'

'I see.' Cassandra glanced about her abstractedly. 'You're right, of course. I didn't want to come here.'

Jay's jaw was taut. 'Are you enjoying this, Cass? Do you get some selfish pleasure out of making me sick with frustration? For God's sake, what do you have to tell me? Is it you? Are you ill or something?' His lips twisted. 'Or is it money? Do you find you're rather short on funds, and think I might be good for a loan?'

'No.' Cassandra stared at him urgently, her knuckles white with the pressure she was putting on them.

'Then what is it?' Jay raised his eyes heavenward. 'What do you want from me? What can you conceivably have to say to me?'

'Can't you guess?' Cassandra took a deep breath. 'I—I'd have rather dealt with this in my own way, but—but Thea insisted you should be told. You see—I'm pregnant!'

CHAPTER EIGHT

THERE was complete silence in the apartment after she had uttered the words, and Cassandra knew an aching sense of relief for having told him at last. It was not what she had wanted to do. She would have much preferred to deal with her pregnancy in her own way. But Thea had insisted, and she had eventually given in.

'I don't agree that a child belongs solely to its mother,' she had told Cassandra quietly. 'Just because a woman has the task of bearing the child around in her body for nine months it doesn't make it any more hers than the father's. Jay has a right to be told. Whatever his faults, he deserves to be given the facts, whether or not he agrees with your decision.'

'But I don't want a baby!' Cassandra had exclaimed fiercely, and Thea had heaved a deep sigh.

'No one can make you do what you don't want, Cass,' she had said gently. 'Just don't make any reckless decisions, until you've spoken to Jay.'

'I won't marry him, you know,' Cassandra had persisted. 'It—it could even be someone else's baby. He'll never know for sure.'

'But you know, and I know,' averred Thea flatly. 'And he also knows you're not the kind of girl who sleeps around.'

'But what's the point of telling him?' Cassandra had protested. 'Thea, if you think there's going to be some romantic reconciliation, you couldn't be more wrong. Jay—Jay's not the type to want a wife and baby hanging round his neck, and so far as I'm concerned the whole affair is an absolute fiasco!'

Liz had been characteristically scornful. Cassandra

123

had not even intended to tell her friend; but the other
girl had arrived at her flat one morning to find
Cassandra being violently sick, and her woman's intui-
tion had supplied the solution.

'Jay Ravek!' she had said, with cold disparagement.
'Oh, Cass, really, how could you?'

But curiously, Cassandra had not wanted to discuss
the matter with Liz, and she had declared somewhat
recklessly that she was not going to have the baby. Liz
had approved, and since then the subject had been
sacrosanct between them.

Now she saw that Jay was pouring himself another
drink, and to avoid watching him, she looked round the
room. It really was a beautiful apartment, she thought
enviously. The comfortable velvet sofas were set at right
angles to a carved chimneypiece, the walls were plain
and hung with Impressionist paintings, and the jewel-
patterned carpet was thick and soft and expensive.

'You're sure?' Jay was speaking to her now, and
Cassandra forced herself to meet his intent gaze.

'Quite sure.'

Jay swallowed the remainder of the liquid in his glass
and replaced it on the tray, his expression dark and
brooding. It had evidently been quite a shock to him,
and she wondered what he was thinking. Perhaps he
would think she had come here for money, after all.
Abortions could be expensive, and she had no doubt
that that was how he would suggest she solve the problem.

Of course, her situation would probably give him a
spurious kind of satisfaction. If he recalled how he had
once offered to marry her, this development should
appeal to his sense of humour. She was glad she needed
nothing from him, she thought fiercely. The humiliation
of asking for his help would have been an ignominy
indeed.

Realising she had done what she came to do, she

turned and reached for her cape, but his voice arrested her. 'What are you doing?'

Cassandra cast him a wary look. 'I'm going,' she replied huskily. 'I've told you now. There's nothing more to be said.'

'Oh, isn't there?' Jay covered the space between them in a couple of seconds. 'You can't expect to come here and tell me something like this and then walk out again without any further explanation!'

'What further explanation is necessary?' Cassandra tilted her chin. 'I'm pregnant. I didn't want to be, but I am. And now I've informed you of the fact, as Thea insisted.'

Jay's eyes glittered. 'You haven't told me what you want from me.'

'What I want from you?' Cassandra shook her head. 'I don't believe I said I wanted anything from you.'

Jay clenched his fists. 'Don't play with words, Cass. What are you going to do? How are you going to have the baby? You'll have to give up your job——'

'Now wait a minute!' Cassandra drew a choking breath. 'I—I haven't said I'm going to have the baby yet——'

Jay's dark eyes narrowed. 'Then why have you come here?'

'I—I've told you, Thea insisted. She—she said you had a right to know——'

'And she was right.' Jay's expression was grim.

'I don't see why.' Cassandra shifted uncertainly. 'I—it's not your problem.'

His lips twisted. 'So what's your solution? An abortion?'

She caught her lower lip between her teeth. 'I—I don't know.' Until that moment, she had not realised how uncertain she really was. Informing Liz that that was her intention had been an act of bravado. To actually contemplate the act of destroying the life that was growing inside her made her feel physically sick.

'Is this some clever ploy?' Jay asked suddenly, and her eyes widened.

'A ploy?' she echoed. 'I—I don't——'

'If it's marriage you want, then why don't you say so?' he demanded. 'At least, be honest with me——'

'Honest with you!' Cassandra knew an angry sense of humiliation. 'Now look here—I didn't want to come here, I didn't want to tell you, I knew how objectionable you would be! As—as for suggesting I might be angling for a proposal——' She broke off emotionally, and had to control her tremulous voice before continuing: 'I—my God! You're so conceited!'

'Not conceited, only practical,' he retorted heavily, and she groped blindly for her cape, needing to get away from him. 'What was your intention then? To make me suffer?'

'To make you suffer?' Cassandra paused to shake her head. 'How could I make you suffer, Jay? You can't pretend you care, one way or the other.'

'And if I do?'

'But—but——' Cassandra stumbled over her words, '—it was an accident, a—a physical error. I mean—I never dreamt, I never thought——' She twisted her hands together. 'After Mike——'

'After Mike, what?' he probed. 'Don't tell me you've never heard of the pill.'

'Of course I've heard of it.' Cassandra was crimson. 'But I've never used it.'

'No?'

'No. It—it wasn't necessary. I mean—well, it was so rarely——'

'All right, you don't have to go on.' Jay heaved a sigh. 'I get the picture. Roland told you you were frigid, and you believed him.'

Cassandra moistened her dry lips and said, almost bemusedly: 'In five years—*in five years*——'

Jay's mouth took on a faintly mocking slant. 'It only takes one night, Cass.' He shook his head. 'I should have known you wouldn't—you hadn't——' He broke off when he saw he was embarrassing her still further, and added quietly: 'How long have you known?'

Cassandra hesitated. 'Does it matter?' Then, aware of his lowering expression: 'For certain—two weeks.'

'Two weeks!' His eyes were calculating. 'I wonder what you would have done if you hadn't come here?'

She shrugged. 'I'd have managed.'

'Really?' Jay took a deep breath. 'Well, you can relax. I will marry you, as no doubt your mother-in-law hoped I would——'

'What?' Cassandra drew back from him in dismay. 'I—I don't want to marry you. I—I don't want to marry anyone.'

'Then you shouldn't get yourself into this kind of a predicament, should you?' he remarked caustically. 'You forget, I'm not as naïve as you are. I know about abortions. I've seen what can happen. Believe me, you wouldn't like it.'

Cassandra trembled. 'You've had that much experience?' she taunted bitterly.

'In the course of my work, yes,' he retorted harshly. 'For God's sake, Cass, you don't think I make a habit of this! What kind of a monster do you think I am?'

She bent her head. 'It's my decision. You can't make up my mind for me.'

'No, I can't,' he agreed tautly. 'But I do tend to think that if you'd intended doing something about it, you'd have done it before now.'

'These things take time to arrange,' protested Cassandra, but Jay merely folded his arms and regarded her with mild contempt. 'In any case, I—I could have the baby without involving you.'

'But you won't,' declared Jay coldly. 'You forget, I know all about being born a bastard, and I have no intention of allowing any son—or daughter—of mine to suffer the same fate.'

Cassandra sought wildly for a means of escape. This wasn't what she wanted. To be tied in matrimony to a man who was only marrying her to legitimise their baby was worse than admitting his previous proposal. At least, then, he had wanted *her*. Now, he coldbloodedly admitted his detachment.

She felt sick. All of a sudden the strain of sustaining this argument in her condition began to take its toll. So far, apart from the morning bouts of nausea, which were pretty ghastly while they lasted, she had felt reasonably healthy, but her weakness today stemmed from the fact that she had eaten no lunch. She felt quite lightheaded looking up at him, and shaking her head, she sank down upon the sofa.

'Are you all right?'

The concern in Jay's voice was disturbing, and she felt ridiculously near to tears. Dear God, she couldn't be ill here, she thought sickly, as a film of sweat broke out upon her forehead. She didn't want his sympathy, artificial as it would be. She should have allowed Thea to come with her, as her mother-in-law had suggested. To face Jay alone had proved too much for her.

Jay was looking down at her with apparent anxiety, and although she was sure it was false, she felt herself responding to it. 'I—I just felt a little dizzy,' she admitted, gripping the arm of the sofa, and then lost the remainder of her colour as she slumped across the cushions.

Cassandra had never fainted in her life, but when she opened her eyes, she realised that that was what must have happened. She was lying down now, on one of the comfortable sofas, a soft velvet pillow cushioning her head; and Jay was squatting beside her.

'You're not all right,' he muttered impatiently, as she

became aware of his presence, and in those first few seconds between unconsciousness and total awareness, Cassandra's heart leapt at the urgency of his tone.

'I—am fine, honestly,' she assured him, trying to sit up, but his hand on her shoulder urged her back. 'I'm perfectly healthy,' she protested, her voice gathering strength. 'I—I just didn't eat any lunch today, and—and I suppose I'm hungry.' She coloured. 'I do get hungry more readily, and—and not at the most convenient times.'

Jay straightened, pushing his hands into the hip pockets of his slacks as he looked down at her. The action tautened the material across his thighs, drawing her unwilling attention to the powerful muscles outlined beneath the cloth. It reminded her of the intimacy they had once shared, and although she dragged her eyes away, she could not deny that physically he had lost none of his appeal. It was so unfair, she thought bitterly, resenting his detachment. He was just as much to blame for her condition, yet he was not in danger of becoming fat and ugly.

'I'll get you something to eat,' he said, glancing at his watch, but Cassandra shook her head.

'There's no need, thank you. I—I'd prefer to go home.' She determinedly swung her feet to the floor. 'If you would just call me a taxi——'

'Not yet.' Jay seated himself on the sofa opposite, his legs spread wide, his hands hanging loosely between. 'We have to talk. There are arrangements to be made. Not least, when you're going to marry me.'

Cassandra moved her shoulders in a helpless gesture. 'You don't want to marry me——'

'I suggest we do it soon,' he continued, almost as if she hadn't spoken. 'As a matter of fact, it coincides very well with certain plans I've made.'

'Plans?' Cassandra was bewildered. 'Jay, why are you doing this?'

He got up from the couch and walked across the room. 'I'm leaving the *Post*,' he said, pushing his hands back into his pockets. Not, as I once told you, to join a television network, but to give myself time to write a book.'

'A book?' She gazed blankly at him.

'Yes, a book,' he agreed drily. 'It's not as outrageous as it sounds. It's something I've been wanting to do for some time and lately—well, lately, I've got a little bored with the kind of life I've been leading.'

Cassandra shook her head. 'And you expect me to help you?'

'No.' He gave her a wry grimace. 'All I'm saying is, I've had it in mind to buy—or lease—a house outside London. Somewhere in—Oxfordshire, perhaps. Somewhere quiet, where I wouldn't get too many visitors.'

Cassandra wetted her lips. 'You—you can't imagine I——'

'—would leave London, too? Oh, yes.' Jay was positive. 'I would say, in your condition, it was an ideal arrangement.'

'You're crazy!'

'Why?'

'It may have slipped your notice, but I have a career of my own.'

He inclined his head. 'It's your own company. Take some time off.'

Cassandra gasped. 'I can't. There only are the two of us.'

'I'm sure Allen could find someone else.'

She couldn't take this in. 'You don't seriously——'

'Oh, yes, I do.' Jay was very serious as he walked back to stand looking down at her. 'I have no intention of leaving you here and running the risk of your having a miscarriage.'

'I can take care of myself!' Cassandra was indignant.

'Can you?' Jay was sceptical.

'Yes.'

She got abruptly to her feet, but as she did so the room revolved alarmingly. She swayed, and immediately Jay's arms caught her, drawing her against him, his fingers at her waist steadying her until the awful giddiness passed.

'You see?' he murmured, close to her ear, and she was made intensely conscious of his nearness and what it was doing to her. 'You just don't know how to look after yourself,' he told her. 'But when we're married, I intend to change all that.'

Cassandra drew away from him, but cautiously this time, risking no revival of that debilitating weakness. 'You can't be serious,' she pleaded. 'You don't really want to marry me.'

'No,' he said at last, his words brutally frank. 'No, I don't want to marry you, but you are carrying my child, and everything else is irrelevant.'

She trembled. 'And—and if I refuse?'

'I could take you to court,' he stated bleakly. 'That would be original, wouldn't it? I should say, without hesitation, it might even warrant national coverage!'

'You—you wouldn't!'

'Wouldn't I?'

Jay's eyes were hostile, and Cassandra shook her head before subsiding on to the sofa again. She was hardly aware of him leaving her, until he returned a few minutes later with a tray of tea and some thin sandwiches. With bland insistence, he put them down on the low table between the sofas, and gestured to Cassandra to help herself.

'My housekeeper always leaves me a snack, even when I'm dining out,' he explained. 'Go ahead. Help yourself.'

'I don't want anything,' Cassandra exclaimed dully, turning her head away, but Jay came down on the sofa beside her and thrust the plate under her nose.

'Don't be a fool,' he said. 'Starving yourself isn't going to solve anything. I promise you, they're good.'

Cassandra could smell ham, and cheese, and the delicious flavour of cucumber, and with a resentful shrug of her shoulders she obediently helped herself to a sandwich. She ate it unwillingly, but she felt so much better afterwards, she took another, and before she knew what she was doing she had eaten more than half of what was on the plate.

'I'm sorry,' she mumbled, swallowing some of the hot tea he had poured her. 'I—I must have been more hungry than I thought. Do—do eat the rest.'

'I'm dining out,' replied Jay flatly, lounging back against the green velvet cushions. 'Please—finish them. Mrs Temple will be highly delighted, I assure you.'

Cassandra put down her teacup. 'You really mean to go ahead with this, don't you?'

Jay nodded.

'Then—then don't you think you're being totally unreasonable?'

'Perhaps.' He was noncommittal.

'Suppose——' Cassandra was hesitant, 'suppose I agree to our getting married.' She paused. 'Don't you think you could—meet me halfway?'

'In what way?'

'By allowing me to stay in London.'

'No.'

'But I can't just—abandon Chris!'

'I'm not asking you to.' Jay's mouth turned down. 'I guess you must be—what? Two months pregnant?'

'Ten weeks, actually,' admitted Cassandra reluctantly.

'Okay. So I'm prepared to allow you another—month to make other arrangements.'

'A month?' Cassandra was appalled.

'I'm being generous,' declared Jay flatly. 'My instincts

tell me to make it a week.'

She bit into another sandwich. 'And—and afterwards? After the baby is born, I mean. I'll—get a divorce?'

'If that's what you want, I can't stop you.'

Thea was undisguisedly delighted by Cassandra's news.

'You knew what he would say, didn't you?' Cassandra accused her hotly. 'Thea, he actually threatened to sue me if I didn't go along with his plans!'

'How could he sue you?' Thea was disarmingly gentle. 'Darling, the man wants to marry you. Be thankful he hasn't washed his hands of the whole affair.'

'Oh, Thea, you're so old-fashioned!' Cassandra felt a helpless sense of frustration. 'A girl doesn't have to get married just because she's pregnant! Not these days. There are loads of one-parent families, and they haven't all had the blessing of some grey-faced registrar!'

'Nevertheless, you'll find it's for the best,' Thea assured her firmly. 'I mean—let's face it, Cass, you're not exactly affluent, are you? How were you going to afford to have this baby?'

'I probably wouldn't,' retorted Cassandra crossly. 'You know what I said.'

'I also know that talking about something and actually doing it are two different things,' averred Thea, with irritating certainty. 'Relax, darling, Jay will make you happy. I know he will.'

Liz took the news very differently.

'You're crazy,' she avowed angrily. 'Letting him blackmail you into marrying him! For goodness' sake, Cass, pull yourself together before it's too late. If there's no baby, what can he do about it?'

Cassandra shook her head. 'I couldn't do that,' she replied. It was strange, she reflected, but whenever anyone tried to give her advice, she tended to swing in the opposite direction. 'I—I'm going to have this baby.'

Liz snorted. 'Well, I think you're mad. Hell, Cass, I thought you said you wanted a career. God knows, I've done everything I can to make it a success. I thought you'd had enough of marriage to last you a lifetime!'

Cassandra had thought so, too, but something drove her to say: 'Jay's not like Mike. He—well, it's different with him.'

'Is it?' Liz's lips curled. 'Well, I have heard he's quite a stud in bed.' She snorted contemptuously. 'You must get his ex-girl-friends to give you the lowdown!'

Cassandra flinched, and needing to strike back, she enquired tersely: 'Including you, Liz?'

Liz gave her a scornful look. 'I wouldn't touch Jay Ravek with a long stick,' she declared, making for the door. 'Goodbye, Cass. You're a fool. And don't come running to me if that louse you found under that stone turns out to be a louse, after all!'

CHAPTER NINE

HONEYSUCKLE Cottage stood on the outskirts of Combe Bassett, about eight miles south-west of Sutton Medlock. Jay said that that was the nearest town, but as Cassandra had never even heard of Sutton Medlock, let alone Combe Bassett, she estimated their whereabouts in relation to Cheltenham, some twenty-five miles away.

It had been an uneasy journey from London, with rain blanketing their surroundings in a chilly mist, and the absence of any familiar landmarks had left Cassandra feeling decidedly anxious. The prospect of the next few months filled her with a mixture of alarm and apprehension, and the realisation that she was Jay's wife now did nothing to ease her sense of isolation.

They had been married that morning, a civil ceremony, at Kensington Register Office, with only Thea and Chris, and some friends of Jay's, the Conways, as witnesses. Cassandra had already met and liked Guy and Helen Conway. She and Helen were much of an age, and as Helen had had a baby herself the year before, they had something in common. Afterwards, they had all had lunch together at the Savoy Grill, and Cassandra thought how incongruous it was to be drinking their health in champagne. Warm milk would have been more appropriate, she thought, bearing in mind the reason for their nuptials.

It was almost six weeks since she had paid that fateful visit to Jay's apartment. Looking back on it now, she felt almost resentful of what had been achieved in such a short time. It was as if fate was conspiring against her, and even Chris had not given her the support she had expected.

'Don't let it worry you,' he had said, when she had broached the subject of her replacement. 'I'll cope. And Combe Bassett's not so far away that I can't ask your advice from time to time.'

'But the work that's already in hand!' Cassandra had protested. 'How will you get through it all?'

'I'll get Paul to help me,' Chris replied airily. 'He's quite astute, as you know, and he's already suggested we advertise for temporary assistance. Art schools are funnelling out talented students all the time. Leave it to us. We'll find someone.'

'But how will you pay them?' Cassandra had wailed. 'Chris, you know we can't afford——'

'We can.' Chris spoke confidently. 'As a matter of fact, I know of someone who's prepared to back us for a while. Stop worrying, Cass. Ro-Allen Interiors is not about to fold.'

Thinking of this now, Cassandra felt a renewed sense of desolation. Ro-Allen had been her idea, her *baby*; the only kind of baby she had ever expected to produce.

She was brought out of her reverie by the sound of Jay slamming the car door, and glancing round, she realised he had got out to open up the boot. The Ferrari was crammed with her belongings, and while he was unloading suitcases and boxes, Cassandra had her first real look at her new home.

It certainly looked more attractive than she had expected from Jay's description. It's just an old country cottage, he had told her, with no central heating, septic tank drainage, and half an acre of land. But it was nearing the end of March, he had added, and if he decided to stay on in the country after the baby was born, he would look around for something a little bigger with more amenities. Cassandra, aware that her baby was due in August, had reserved judgment. But she had had little belief that she would be spending next winter in Combe Bassett.

'Do you need any help, Mrs Ravek?'

As Cassandra pushed open her door to get out, a woman in her fifties emerged from the cottage and came down the garden path to greet them. Cassandra had already met Mrs Temple, and it was somewhat of a relief to see at least one familiar face.

'I can manage,' she said now, closing the car door behind her and swaying for a moment in the damp evening air. It had been quite a mild day in London, the rain holding off until they had stepped into the car, but it was much cooler now and Cassandra shivered.

'Go along inside,' directed Mrs Temple firmly, noticing the girl's sudden pallor. 'There's a warm fire in the drawing room, and a drink, too, if you'd like one. If not, I've a kettle boiling in the kitchen, and it won't take a minute to brew some tea.'

'Tea would be lovely,' agreed Cassandra, glancing round. 'Here, let me take that suitcase.'

'Leave it!' said Jay authoritatively, straightening from the boot. 'Do as Mrs Temple says. Go and get warm. You don't want to spend your first few days here recovering from the 'flu, do you?'

Cassandra was tempted to argue, but with Mrs Temple looking on she acquiesced. But she wasn't a child, and she didn't like being treated like one, particularly in the circumstances.

It was obvious why the cottage had been so named, and she ducked beneath the drooping vine to gain access to a stone-flagged porch. Beyond, a panelled hallway smelt deliciously of lavender, and as she stepped inside she realised the cottage was bigger than she had thought.

Several doors opened from the hall, all closed but one, and when she glanced into the open aperture, she guessed this was the drawing room Mrs Temple had spoken of. The carpets in the hall, and in this room, whose windows overlooked the lane in front of the cottage, were surprisingly new for a rented property, and the furniture that gave the drawing room a comfortable elegance, did not look like the worn possessions of a retiring couple. But the squashy chintz-covered sofa and easy chairs were evidently not from Jay's apartment, and Cassandra came to the conclusion that Helen's aunt and uncle must have refurnished quite recently.

She was still hovering in the doorway, surveying the cosy room with its large open fire, when Jay came into the hall. She heard the sound of his footsteps and stiffened instinctively, but after a moment they receded again as he continued on upstairs. She looked out of the door tentatively as Mrs Temple followed her employer inside, and the housekeeper pulled a face as she set her burden down.

'Go and sit down, Mrs Ravek,' she exclaimed, as Cassandra's eyes turned reluctantly from the right-angled curve of the staircase. 'I'll go and make the tea before I take these boxes upstairs. You'll be happy to know your books arrived yesterday, and I've left them in the study for you to unpack.'

Cassandra loosened the jacket of the cream silk suit she had worn to be married in. 'Really, Mrs Temple,' she said carefully, 'I'm not an invalid, you know. Just show me where the kitchen is, and I'll make the tea. I don't want you to think I intend to spend my days in idleness.'

Mrs Temple hestiated. 'Mr Ravek——'

'Mr Ravek isn't here at this moment,' declared Cassandra, albeit lowering her tone. 'Come on, Mrs Temple. I'd really like to help. Just tell me what you want me to do and I'll do it.'

Mrs Temple gave in unwillingly. 'Well, the kitchen's through there, Mrs Ravek. Like I said, the tea's just waiting to be brewed. But I won't be a minute taking these things upstairs, and if there's anything you're not sure of, just you let me know.'

Cassandra smiled. 'I'm quite sure making a pot of tea won't overtax my capabilities,' she remarked drily. 'You'll join us, won't you, Mrs Temple? I'm sure Jay will have instructions for you.'

In truth, Cassandra wanted to delay the moment when she and Jay would be alone together, and she had yet to discover what the sleeping arrangements would be.

The square kitchen at the back of the cottage was remarkably well equipped. The stone floor had been softened by the introduction of brick-coloured rubber tiles, and against the rosy-pink walls was set an assortment of labour-saving devices. Cassandra was again surprised. She had expected an old-fashioned gas cooker and little else. Instead, she saw a split-level oven with rotary spit, a fridge-freezer, which would accommodate the food for a family, an automatic washing machine and tumble drier, and even a medium-sized dishwasher. Certainly, Mrs Temple would have nothing to complain about here, particularly as the room was warmed by an Aga boiler, whose glowing eye took away any feeling of having walked into a showroom window.

Mrs Temple had left a tray on the table, that occupied the middle of the floor. Two teacups, a milkjug and sugar basin, and a teapot, sat beside a plate of home-made scones and some delicious fruit cake, and Cassandra's tummy gurgled in anticipation of the food.

The electric kettle soon boiled, and after filling the pot, Cassandra looked round for a third cup. She was opening the third cupboard door when Mrs Temple came in, and she felt her colour rising in spite of herself as she explained what she was looking for.

'All the teacups are in here, Mrs Ravek,' the house-keeper explained, apparently without objection, opening the sliding cupboard above a melamine working surface.

'But don't you worry about me. I'll make my own tea and have it in here, if you don't mind. I'd rather. You and I can have a proper chat some other time, when Mr Ravek is working.'

Cassandra opened her mouth to protest, but Mrs Temple had turned away, and with a feeling of inevitability, she picked up the tray. After all, she couldn't go on relying on Mrs Temple as a kind of mediator between them. She had married Jay, and somehow she had to learn his kind of detachment.

There was no one in the drawing room when Cassandra carried the tray through from the kitchen. She set it down on the low table beside the couch, but she had scarcely time to breathe a sigh of relief before she heard Jay coming down the stairs.

He came into the room vigorously, bringing with him a feeling of energy and vitality, and Cassandra thought again how unfair it was that they were equally responsible for the child inside her, and yet she was expected to bear all the hardship.

He had shed his jacket, she saw, as he closed the door behind him and came to join her on the hearth. He had worn a dark grey three-piece suit to get married in, and now he had taken off his tie and unloosened the top two buttons of his shirt. With his hair slightly ruffled from his exertions, and drops of rain sparkling among the dark strands, he looked relaxed and approachable, and Cassandra's pulses tingled at the unwilling awareness that this relationship had its compensations.

'Why don't you sit down and make a start?' he suggested, glancing round thoughtfully, before making his way across the room to where a tray of drinks invited his inspection. 'I need something stronger than tea. What do you have in those cases? Armour?'

Cassandra's lips parted humorously, and without trying to anticipate future developments, she sat down on the couch and helped herself to a scone. They were delicious, and unable to resist, she had another, raising her eyes to meet his intent gaze without thinking.

'You look like a little girl caught stealing cream cakes,' he remarked, with disturbing emphasis. 'Go ahead—make a pig of yourself. I like you better with a bit of flesh on your bones.'

Cassandra put down the second scone at once. 'You mean I'm getting fat,' she accused, her appetite affected as much by his tone as by what he had said.

'I mean you've lost that waiflike air,' he retorted firmly. 'Don't look so put out. It suits you.'

Cassandra made no move to eat anything else. It was bad enough knowing she couldn't help gaining a certain amount of weight over the next few months, without adding to her predicament by over-eating.

Jay sighed, noticing her self-absorption, and came to join her on the couch. 'What's wrong?' he asked, his dark eyes unexpectedly gentle. 'You've hardly said a word since we left London. You're not still mad at me, are you? I thought we'd got over all that.'

She stiffened. 'Why? Because I seem to have fallen in with all your plans? Because I haven't interfered with any of your arrangements?' She bent her head. 'I didn't think there was much point. You made your position perfectly clear.'

'Cass!' His use of her name was exasperated. 'Cass, what's brought all this on? I thought we agreed it was best—for all of us. You know perfectly well you could never have gone through with an abortion.'

'What do you mean?' She looked indignantly up at him.

'I mean what I say,' averred Jay flatly. He shook his head. 'Honey, you may think you're very cool and emancipated, but I know better. You're not the type. You're not like—Liz Lester, say. She wouldn't have hesitated, and she certainly wouldn't have bothered to tell the father of her child what she intended.'

Cassandra's long lashes flicked upward. 'You say that with confidence. Have you had personal experience?' she enquired impulsively, and then blushed at the realisation of what she had said. 'I'm sorry,' she muttered, looking away. 'Don't answer that. It's nothing to do with me. I don't know what I was thinking——'

Jay took one of the silver-blonde curls that had now reached her shoulder, and tugged on it insistently. 'I don't mind you asking,' he assured her solemnly. 'And just for the record, Liz and I didn't have that kind of relationship.'

Her face burned. 'As I said, it's nothing to do with me.'

'Maybe not.' Jay shrugged, finishing his scotch. 'But I thought I'd tell you anyway. Now, why don't you have a piece of Mrs Temple's fruit cake? I can assure you it's delicious.'

Cassandra shook her head. 'I've had enough. You have some.' She slanted a sideways look at him. 'You don't look as if you need to diet.'

'Nor do you,' responded Jay patiently. 'Cass, at the risk of sounding trite, let me say you've never looked more beautiful than you do right now. Being pregnant suits you.' His lips tightened. 'But now, if you insist on behaving melodramatically, I suggest you allow me to show you where you're going to sleep.'

'It's all right for you,' declared Cassandra, disbelieving him and getting to her feet. 'You don't have to contemplate the future in terms of tent-like dresses and vitamin pills, and bumping into things because you're big and clumsy!'

Jay regarded her with sudden understanding. 'Is that how you see it?' he asked quietly. 'Just as—an awful nuisance?'

Cassandra went past him. 'How else do you expect me to see it?' she exclaimed, refusing to respond to the almost irresistible appeal of his voice. 'Which way do we go? Upstairs, I suppose. Perhaps you'd better lead the way, as you've been here before.'

Jay said nothing more. He set down his glass and preceded her out of the room, leading the way towards the stairs without further hesitation. He was obviously angry, but Cassandra refused to feel contrite. What else did he expect? she thought, justifying her belligerence. She hadn't wanted to come here, and just because she had to give in, it did not mean she now must endorse all his arrangements.

There were three bedrooms, Cassandra discovered, much to her relief, but only one bathroom. Like downstairs, however, all the rooms were attractively furnished, and breaking their silence she commented on this.

'The Mortons put most of their furniture into store,' Jay explained brusquely. 'It was pretty old stuff, and they had no objection. I had a firm from London come and look the cottage over. They liased with a store in Sutton Medlock to have the whole place fitted out in keeping with its character. I thought you would approve.'

'Well, I do.' But Cassandra knew she sounded grudging. 'Er—what firm from London?'

'Ro-Allen Interiors,' replied Jay offhandedly, ignoring her gasp of disbelief. 'I thought it might help to widen their horizons, and any kind of advertising is good news.'

She felt awful. 'Why didn't you tell me?'

'It was supposed to be a surprise,' said Jay flatly. 'Now, which room do you prefer? I see Mrs Temple has put your things in the back room, but if you'd prefer the front——'

'Oh, Jay!'

Cassandra gazed at him helplessly. She didn't know what to say. The trouble was, whatever she said would sound counterfeit now, and she turned abruptly and walked into the back bedroom.

Unlike the front, which was principally designed in shades of green and beige, the back was all cream and gold, with a fluffy cream carpet and a thick cream velvet spread. The furniture was composed of reproduction pieces, many of which were gilt-edged, and the heavy curtains at the leaded windows were of gold-tasselled brocade.

Jay had turned on the gold-shaded lamp beside the bed, giving the room an added warmth, and in spite of the fact that there was no central heating, the room did not feel cold. Cassandra walked to the window and looked out on to undulating fields and a dark copse of trees, and knew an unexpected sense of wellbeing. She couldn't be glad she was here, she told herself fiercely, but the fact remained, she did feel an insidious contentment stealing over her.

'Do you like it?'

When Jay spoke she realised he had come to stand behind her, and her pulses raced in spite of herself. 'I—it's beautiful,' she conceded, keeping her back to him. 'I really am grateful, even if—even if——'

'—even if you didn't want to come here, I know,' he finished laconically, but Cassandra shook her head.

'No, I—that's not what I meant.' She licked her dry lips. 'I was just about to say—even if I don't—don't always show it.'

'I see.' Jay exhaled slowly, the warmth of his breath moving the hair at her nape. 'Well, believe it or not, I do want you to be happy here.'

Cassandra breathed shallowly. 'Yes.'

He hesitated. 'So—are you going to forgive me? For forcing you into this?'

She sighed. 'I'd rather not talk about it.'

'Why not?' Jay's hands were suddenly at her thickening waistline, and before she could guess his intentions, he had drawn her back against him. 'Cass, you know

what I want,' he said unsteadily. 'You know what holding you like this is doing to me. We're married, Cass.
What's to stop us from leading a normal existence, from
living together like any other husband and wife——'

'Don't!' With a shudder of self-revulsion for the desperate urge she experienced to give in to his plea,
Cassandra pulled herself away from him. 'Please,' she
choked, keeping herself stiff and unresponsive. 'You
know why we're married. And—and you know I intend
to get a divorce as soon as—as soon as it's over. What—
what you're suggesting is—is impossible!'

Jay swung her round to face him. 'Why is it impossible?' he demanded, but his gentleness had gone and
she could see the light of hostility in his eyes. 'What are
you afraid of now, Cass? Me? Or yourself? Maybe
Roland deserved some sympathy after all. God knows,
if you froze him off as you're freezing me, perhaps he
was justified in seeking consolation elsewhere!'

Cassandra slept badly that night. She was intensely conscious of Jay sleeping in the room across the landing;
and while she could console herself with the thought
that he was unlikely to make any further overtures towards her, she was painfully aware that it wasn't quite
that simple.

The truth was, she had wanted to give in to him. She
had wanted to accept his invitation and pretend their
marriage was something it was not. But that was all it
would have been—*pretence*; and once the child was
born, there would be no further reason for that convenient charade.

Nevertheless, lying there in the darkness, so much
darker than she was used to in London, Cassandra had
to concede the idea had some merit. Jay wanted her,
and God knew, she wanted him; she wanted his warmth
and protection, she wanted the pulsating strength of his
manhood, and the wild, mindless ecstasy of his posses-

sion. But she wanted his love, too, and love was something Jay didn't talk about. He talked about wanting and needing, and living together; but never love. And love was something Cassandra needed, not least because she had discovered she was in love with her husband! Crazy though it might seem, and against all the odds, she had been unable to resist it at the last, and their living together was going to be sufficient torment as it was, without the ever-present knowledge that if she did allow him to get close to her, she was inviting self-destruction. Jay was not the kind of man to settle down to married life. He had never pretended otherwise. So somehow she was going to have to get through these weeks and months without disclosing her ever-present weakness.

CHAPTER TEN

CASSANDRA was lying down in her bedroom when she heard Jay go out. She heard the sound of the porch door as it slammed behind him, and guessed that Mrs Temple had the back door open, too, causing the sudden vacuum. It was a hot afternoon, and it was impossible to get enough air into the house, and Cassandra had gone to lie down only because it enabled her to take off all her clothes.

Now, almost compulsively, she levered herself up from the bed and wrapping a cotton gown around her, opened the bedroom door. The landing window gave a view of the drive that ran along the side of the cottage, and presently she was rewarded by the sight of her husband reversing the Ferrari out into the lane. The powerful car swung round in a half circle before Jay thrust the engine into forward gear and accelerated away, leaving a cloud of dust hanging in the air behind him.

Cassandra sighed. She wondered where Jay was going. He had started going out a lot recently, and when he came back it was usually too late for him to discuss with her where he had been. Perhaps he had another woman, she reflected tautly, aware that this idea was coming more frequently to her lately. After all, how could she blame him? He was a normal healthy male, and it was three months since they had left London.

Three months! Cassandra turned and walked back into her bedroom, running an exploring hand over the swollen mound of her stomach. In spite of all her fears, the time was passing, and what had seemed a lifetime no longer looked that way.

On the contrary, the weeks were passing more quickly than she would have believed possible, and she had been amazed at how smoothly they had settled into a routine. Mrs Temple had been a boon of course, and her presence had ironed out some of the more awkward moments. But, nevertheless, she had Jay to thank for making things easy for her, Jay, whose calm tolerance and facile humour had oiled the wheels of matrimony.

Not that she could truly regard their arrangement as a marriage. Apart from that one occasion, the day of the wedding, Jay had never referred to the physical side of their relationship, and although they lived in the same house and shared the same meals, their association was emotionally detached. They were companions, nothing more, two people brought together by circumstance, and without any real means of communication.

In the beginning, Cassandra had welcomed this development. She had been relieved when Jay announced that he intended to start work on his book immediately, and every morning he disappeared into the study downstairs, and only joined her for lunch. The afternoons had been much the same, until recently, and Cassandra had got used to accompanying Mrs Temple on her shopping trips into the village, and enjoying the new sensation of becoming a part of village life.

But latterly, Cassandra had begun to wish Jay would pay a little more attention to her. She missed having a man to talk to, and her infrequent telephone conversations with Chris in no way made up for a verbal combat of words. On the rare evenings when he did join her after dinner, his nose was invariably buried in a book, and when she did arouse a comment from him, he was always infuriatingly polite.

What was wrong with her? she asked herself now, shedding the cotton wrapper and surveying her reflection in the long cheval mirror. She couldn't conceivably expect Jay to feel attracted to her like this, and she always took good care never to appear before him without being suitably covered.

Sighing, she tugged disconsolately at the damp strands of silky blonde hair that clung to her neck. It was so hot, the hottest June on record, she felt sure. And she was forced to wear all-concealing smocks and full-waisted dresses, instead of the bikinis lying useless in the drawer.

Of course, she reflected, it would be much hotter in London, and no doubt Thea thought she was very rude for not inviting her down for a weekend. But the truth was, they had no room, not unless she turned Mrs Temple out of her bedroom, and she couldn't do that. If only she still had her flat, she thought dejectedly. She could have gone up to London and spent a few days with Thea. But although she had insisted on keeping her furniture and putting it into storage, it would have been madness to go on paying the rent for the flat. Besides, she acknowledged now, Jay might not have approved of her going away, and the last thing she wanted was to rock this uncertain craft.

Even so, she could not help the feeling of abandonment that was gripping her. Where had Jay gone? Why didn't he talk to her about it? Surely if it was something to do with his book, she might be able to help. She would welcome the chance to exercise her intelligence.

Shaking her head, she walked out of the bedroom and into the bathroom, uncaring of her nudity. There was no one to see her except Mrs Temple, and the housekeeper was unlikely to be shocked.

A cold shower left her feeling somewhat brighter,

and after putting on a pretty sprigged cotton smock dress with a camisole bodice, she regarded her appearance with more enthusiasm. She didn't look too repulsive, she decided indifferently, totally unaware that she had never looked lovelier. With the bloom of health in her cheeks and the honey-gold warmth of the sun colouring her skin, she had a shining natural beauty. And the tumbling silver-blonde waves that now hung almost to her shoulders only enhanced her image.

As she went downstairs, she wondered if Jay had remembered she had to see Doctor Lomax the following day. The doctor, whose surgery was in Sutton Medlock, had no idea that she and Jay were not the happily married couple they appeared to be. Jay always behaved immaculately when they were in his company, and she wondered now what the doctor would say if he knew their real circumstances. She supposed the fact that Jay always escorted her encouraged Doctor Lomax's belief. And although she had had the little Alfa delivered to the cottage, the occasions when she had used it could be counted on one hand.

Perhaps that was what she should do now, she thought—go for a drive on her own. But the unwilling suspicion that Jay might think she was spying on him made her discard the idea, and she walked into the kitchen instead.

Mrs Temple was not indoors, however. She was sitting in a striped deckchair in the garden, which was presently a glorious mass of colour. The Mortons' gardener had continued to come and work for Jay, and the wide expanse of lawn was neatly cut and prettily edged with borders of shrubs and flowers.

Mrs Temple smiled when she saw Cassandra, but as she started to get up, Cassandra waved her back. 'Stay where you are,' she said. 'You look so comfortable.'

'Oh, I am.' Mrs Temple looked about her contentedly.

'Who wouldn't be here? I'm so glad Mr Ravek decided to move out of London.'

'Yes.' Cassandra was noncommittal. 'I—er—Jay's gone out, hasn't he? I—I heard the car.'

'Yes. He left about half an hour ago,' agreed the housekeeper, nodding. 'Didn't say where he was going, but I expect it's to do with that book of his.'

This was Mrs Temple's way of reassuring her, Cassandra knew, and although she was grateful to the housekeeper for her understanding, she couldn't help a sudden irritation with Jay for making this conversation necessary.

'I—er—I think I'll go and get myself some orange juice,' she declared, turning back towards the house. 'You take it easy, Mrs Temple. I know where it is.'

The kitchen, which had felt warm on her way outside, now felt delightfully cool, and the jug of freshly-squeezed orange juice she took from the fridge chilled her fingers. She poured herself a glass and replaced the jug in the fridge, but then, instead of going outside again, she wandered through to the front of the cottage.

Just as the dining room formed a rectangle with the kitchen at the back of the house, the study matched the drawing room across the hall. Although she had entered it a couple of times just after their arrival, lately Cassandra had felt loath to go into the study. It was where Jay worked. She had grown used to hearing the muted clatter of his typewriter through the door, and in spite of the fact that Mrs Temple had stored her books in there, she had felt herself an interloper. In consequence, the study had become very much Jay's domain, and even though he was out now, she was reluctant to intrude.

But boredom, and an unwilling acknowledgment of a sense of curiosity, made her hesitate now at the door, and with a determined shrug of indifference she decisively turned the handle.

Her first impression was of the untidiness of the place. The floor was literally strewn with rolled up balls of paper, not just around the desk, but even in the corners of the room, as if Jay had thrown them there with real force. The desk, too, was spread with discarded sheets of typing paper, carbons and erasing pencils adding to the confusion.

Cassandra shook her head bewilderedly, her own problems forgotten as she took in this unmistakeable evidence of Jay's frustration. It was obvious he was far from satisfied with what he was doing, and she felt only a mild sense of trespass as she picked up some of the curls of paper and opened them out.

Pages of half-typed manuscript met her troubled gaze, lines composed of disjointed phrases and sentences, without any style or originality. The writing was flat, unimaginative, and while the content was impressive, it was totally unlike the incisive brilliance of his work in journalism.

Cassandra had read some of his work now. Before her marriage, Chris had given her several reports to read, filched from a friend in the newsroom at the *Post*, and she had found his writing totally absorbing. She would have discussed it with him, if he had given her half a chance, but somehow it was a personal thing and could not easily be broached.

Now, however, her brow furrowed as she picked up more pages and saw the stumbling etymology repeated. Was this why Jay was spending more and more time away from the cottage? she wondered compassionately. Because the task he had set himself was tearing him to pieces?

Hardly thinking what she was doing, Cassandra gathered all the balls of paper together and deposited them in the waste basket. Then she tidied the desk, dropping pens and pencils into an empty jar and putting all the loose sheets together in a filing tray she found in one of the drawers. Within five minutes the room had assumed some semblance of neatness, and she hoped Jay would find his work easier in more orderly surroundings.

As had happened recently when Jay went out, Cassandra had dinner alone that evening, and she had retired to bed before she heard the sound of the Ferrari pass the cottage on its way to the garage. A quick glance at the clock on the bedside cabinet informed her it was after eleven o'clock, and the book in her hands sagged as she felt the familiar sense of dejection. He had obviously not been researching his book this late in the evening, and her stomach plunged unpleasantly at the obvious explanation.

When she heard him coming upstairs some time later, she was tempted to put out her light. But she doubted he would care whether she was asleep or awake, and pressing her lips together she forced her attention to the words on the page in front of her.

She was totally unprepared for her bedroom door to be flung open, or for Jay to appear in the aperture, and her hand went automatically to her throat as he stood there swaying in the doorway. He was drunk, she realised disbelievingly. Even without the overpowering scent of alcohol about him, she would have known it from the unsteady stance he had adopted and the bloodshot insolence in his eyes.

'Well, well,' he said, making no attempt to moderate his tone. 'How cosy! The little wife staying obediently at home, waiting for her husband's safe return.'

Cassandra hesitated only a moment before reaching for her dressing gown and sliding out of bed. The folds of apricot-coloured silk were hardly concealing, but right now she was more concerned with not waking Mrs Temple.

'Jay——' she began, but he was not listening to

her. His blurred gaze was on her body, ruthlessly appraising her ripe fullness, and she wrapped her arms about herself defensively, unable to pretend she didn't care.

'My child,' Jay said thickly, lifting his eyes to hers. 'My seed there inside you. Be thankful for its protection. A few moments ago I wanted to strangle you!'

Cassandra shook her head helplessly. 'Jay—Jay, it's after eleven——'

'I know what time it is,' he muttered savagely. 'My God, don't I count every minute of every day wishing it was my last?' He pushed his fingers through his hair and gazed at her broodingly. 'And what do you do? You don't even grant me the courtesy of finding my private road to hell!'

'What are you talking about? Cassandra was totally confused. 'Jay—please! I beg of you! Don't make a scene now, not when Mrs Temple is asleep. Whatever it is, can't it wait until morning?'

'Who gave you permission to touch my manuscript?' Jay persisted, and suddenly Cassandra understood. He had been into the study. He had discovered what she had done—and he resented her for it.

'Go to bed, Jay,' she said quietly, taking his arm and propelling him out on to the landing. 'We'll talk about it tomorrow——'

'Like hell we will,' he muttered, tripping in spite of himself and almost taking her with him as he lurched across the top of the stairs.

'Oh, Jay!'

Cassandra made a frustrated sound and pushed open his bedroom door, and as she did so, he stumbled past her and flopped down on to the end of the bed. 'Poking about in the study,' he mumbled, pulling off his tie. 'What were you looking for? What did you hope to find? Whatever it was, I guess you didn't find it amongst that shit!'

Cassandra sighed, and realising Mrs Temple might open her door at any time to see what was going on, she went into Jay's bedroom and half closed the door. 'All right,' she said. 'I admit it was me who tidied up the study. But I wasn't prying, as you seem to think. What you do in there is no concern of mine. But if it was so secret, you should have made sure you didn't leave anything lying about, shouldn't you?'

Jay tugged at the buttons of his shirt. 'So now you know,' he muttered, regarding her with dark hostility. 'I'm as much a failure at that as I am at everything else!'

Cassandra shook her head. 'You're not a failure, and you know it. For some reason you haven't found the right formula, that's all. It'll come. Just give it time.'

'Do you think so?' Jay's tone was derisive. 'Well, who knows? What does it matter anyway? I can always go back to journalism. Perhaps I should never have left it. Perhaps that's the only kind of writing I can do.'

He seemed to be having difficulties with his shirt buttons, and almost instinctively Cassandra went to help him. 'You're just feeling sorry for yourself,' she declared, scarcely realising what she was doing. 'And getting drunk isn't going to improve things. Unless you were serious about trying to kill yourself.'

'Oh, I was serious all right,' murmured Jay softly, looking up at her. 'Living here with you, sleeping under the same roof—you don't know what it's doing to me. I want *you*, Cass, not inspiration!'

Cassandra quivered as his hands touched her, his fingers sliding over her hips, drawing her between his legs. For a moment she was too bemused to do anything, and he pressed his face to the swelling mound of her stomach and shuddered as if he had achieved some desperately needed goal.

'Jay——'

Putting her hands on his shoulders, she tried to move away, but he wouldn't let her go, and besides, as he continued to hold her, she felt an insidious desire to stay where she was expanding inside her.

'Stay with me, Cass,' he muttered, getting up from the bed to gather her fully against him. 'Stay with me . . .'

Cassandra took a trembling breath. 'I—I can't——'

'Why can't you?'

'Jay, this is crazy——'

'No, it's sane,' he told her huskily. 'Cass, if you have any thought for my sanity at all, don't leave me now——'

The sound of Mrs Temple talking to the milkman awakened Cassandra. She lay for several minutes listening to the unusual sound and wondering why she had never noticed it on other mornings, before realising she was not in her own bed. This room was not her room, it was Jay's, and a feeling of shame swept over her as she remembered what had happened.

She had not wanted to give in, but Jay had seemed so vulnerable somehow. It was strange; she had wanted to be strong, but his weakness had overcome her, and when his mouth had parted her lips, it had proved irresistible.

She had thought he would be repulsed by her, but he had not been. He had told her she was foolish to think that way, that she was just as beautiful as ever, and that he had never known such pleasure with anyone else but her.

So she had gone to bed with him, she had let him make love to her, rejoicing in the hard urgency of his body, the thrusting strength of his manhood, that aroused such mindless sweetness inside her. Her limbs

had quivered beneath his possessive hands, her skin had tingled with the abrasive caress of his tongue, and her body had surged against him, seeking the satisfaction only he could give her . . .

She shivered. What had got into her? How could she have given in to nothing more than a physical need? And what kind of precedent had she created? Jay would know now her desire to keep him at bay stemmed from her own need and not his.

She turned her head unwillingly, dreading the thought that he might be watching her, and discovered she was alone in the bed. And why not? It was almost ten o'clock. Jay had gone. His clothes had gone, rescued from the floor where he had abandoned them the night before, and even her nightgown had been picked up and tossed with her dressing gown across the bottom of the bed.

She realised at once she was naked under the sheet, and scrambled up quickly to pull on the silk nightgown. Jay was up, which would account for the fact that Mrs Temple had made no attempt to lower her tone when speaking to the milkman, and presently she was going to fetch Cassandra some tea upstairs, expecting her to be in her own room.

She thrust her legs out of the bed with sudden reluctance. Moving had made her aware of the delicious sense of lethargy that had enveloped her, and her eyelids felt heavy and still full of sleep. Maybe she could go back to sleep again, she reflected dully, desperate to avoid Jay after what had happened, and gathering up her dressing gown, she scurried back to her own room.

But when her tea arrived, it was Jay himself who brought it, not Mrs Temple. He came into her room, frowning at the evident transition, glancing behind him impatiently as if measuring the distance between the two beds.

'Why?' he asked flatly, as she struggled up against the pillows with pink cheeks. 'Wasn't my bed comfortable? Or were you afraid Mrs Temple might throw up her hands at the sight of a wife in her husband's room?'

Cassandra took the tray he had brought and set it firmly across her knees. 'I—I just thought it would look—odd,' she confessed, avoiding his eyes. 'I—thank you for the tea. Mrs Temple couldn't have done better.'

'Mrs Temple prepared it,' stated Jay shortly, pushing his hands into the pockets of his tight-fitting jeans. 'Cass, I offered to bring it up because I wanted to talk to you. And—well, I thought we might talk easier here, away from unwary eavesdroppers.'

'There's no need, really.' Cassandra concentrated on the tray, picking up the lid of the butter dish and toying with the corner of a triangle of toast. 'I—what time did you get up? Was it early? I'm afraid I've overslept. It's after ten——'

'Cass!' Jay came down on the side of the bed, his weight depressing the springs and causing her to hold on to the tray. 'Cass,' he said again, 'I'm sorry. I don't know how to say this, but I do know how you must feel. I was drunk. I behaved like a heel. I swore to myself I'd never take advantage of you, and now I have!'

Cassandra endeavoured to school her features. He blamed *himself*! She could hardly credit it. She had believed she was to blame. If she had not interfered with his manuscript, if she had not gone into his bedroom——

'I guess it was just seeing you like that,' Jay was continuing, smoothing his palms over the worn knees of his trousers. 'I lost my head.' He moved his shoulders. 'You have every reason to despise me.'

Cassandra moistened her lips. 'I—don't despise you,

Jay.' She couldn't be dishonest. 'I—I can't let you take all the blame.'

Jay snorted. 'I could have hurt you!'

'I don't think so.'

His eyes narrowed. 'I always understood—well, a woman had to take care——'

'You didn't hurt me, Jay.' Cassandra held up her head. 'And I'm sorry for disturbing the papers in the study. It was none of my business, and——'

'Forget it.' He got abruptly up from the bed, massaging the back of his neck half impatiently. 'As a matter of fact, that was something else I came to tell you.' He paused. 'It was the book that got me up this morning. I guess it was around six.' He made a rueful gesture. 'Perhaps it was just as well.' His eyes darkened. 'Waking up beside you, I might have had even more to reproach myself for.' He drew a deep breath. 'Anyway, as I say, I got up about six—I don't know why. I just knew I had to go and write, and I suppose now I've typed about five thousand words. It's pretty rough yet. It needs polishing. But—well, I know it's good.'

'Oh, Jay!' Cassandra was genuinely delighted. 'I'm so glad for you.'

'Yes.' Jay's tongue circled his lips. 'I'm pretty glad myself. I can't be absolutely certain, of course, but it feels like I've found the right formula at last. You were right, it was only a matter of time.'

Cassandra forced a smile. 'It's wonderful news!'

'Isn't it?' Jay surveyed her intently. 'So—I guess I'd better go and do some more.'

'Yes.' It was an effort to drag her eyes away, but she managed it, determinedly pouring herself a cup of tea from the silver pot on the tray. She could not put what had happened between them the night before out of her mind, and there was a traitorous yearning inside her to tell him she had changed her mind, that if he still wanted it, she was prepared to make their marriage a proper one, in every way.

'It won't happen again, I promise.' She was just congratulating herself on having achieved a certain measure of composure when the strangled words were torn from Jay's throat. 'You don't have to worry. I have no intention of jeopardising your health—or the health of the child—just to satisfy my sordid desire for your body. I'm sorry. I know it's inadequate, but I am sorry.' He grasped the handle of the door and swung it open. 'Now, eat your breakfast. I haven't forgotten that today's the day you visit Doctor Lomax.'

CHAPTER ELEVEN

IF Cassandra had seen little of Jay before, she saw even less of him now. The sound of his typewriter reverberated in the study from dawn till dusk, and sometimes even later. He was like a man possessed, emerging from his retreat only when bodily needs demanded it, and Cassandra's initial relief gave way to a growing resentment. It was totally unjustified, she knew that. This was the situation as she had anticipated it, and she had no cause for complaint. But since that night in June when she had shared his bed, her feelings towards him had changed; and while she still outwardly clung to the arrangement as it was inaugurated, deep down inside her, other forces were at work. More and more frequently she knew the urge to take the initiative, to go to Jay and demand that he start treating her as a woman, and not as some fragile object that might fall apart in his hands; and more and more frequently she lay awake, long after the house had gone quiet, wondering if her future peace of mind was worth all these wasted nights.

One morning towards the end of July, Jay's mother rang. Lady Fielding had telephoned before, but invariably Jay had taken the call, and Cassandra's knowledge of her mother-in-law was limited to the polite words of greeting exchanged at long distance. Jay had admitted that he and his mother had seldom seen a lot of one another, which would account, Cassandra supposed, for the fact that Lady Fielding had not been invited to the wedding. But *she* had been curious, and she would have welcomed the opportunity to learn more about her husband's family.

On this occasion, however, Jay was not there to answer his mother's call. Mrs Temple had decided to use some of the raspberries going to waste in the garden to make some jam, ·but she had no preserving jars. Unfortunately, the village store did not stock such things, and with some reluctance Jay had agreed to drive into Sutton Medlock and collect a dozen for her. Cassandra would have offered to go with him, but the day was enervating, the sky brassy and ominous, threatening a storm later.

She was sitting in the garden shelling some peas, when the telephone rang. Mrs Temple answered it, but when she came to tell her that Lady Fielding was on the line, Cassandra got up at once to take the call.

'Cassandra?' Jay's mother's voice sounded remarkably near. 'I understand James is not at home.'

'No, that's right.' Cassandra hesitated. 'He's gone into Sutton Medlock for some preserving jars for Mrs Temple. I'm afraid I don't know exactly when he'll be back.'

'Preserving jars? How quaint!' Lady Fielding sounded amused. 'That doesn't sound like James at all.'

Cassandra chuckled, too. 'Well, he wasn't very enthusiastic about going,' she admitted. 'But Mrs Temple can be very persuasive.'

'Ah, yes, Mrs Temple.' The older woman sounded as if she understood. 'Hmm—well, and how are you, my dear? Up to entertaining a couple of visitors, I hope. Giles and I have been staying with some friends in Worcester, and I thought we might make a detour home to come and have lunch with you.'

'To—to have lunch with us?' Cassandra was taken aback.

'Yes, dear. You don't have any objection, do you? I mean, I think it's time I met my daughter-in-law face to face, don't you?'

'I—well—yes. Yes, I suppose so.' Cassandra glanced

round helplessly, wishing Mrs Temple was around to confer with. What would Jay say if she invited his mother and stepfather without his permission? Oh, why had he had to go out this morning of all mornings! 'It's just that—well, I never expected——'

'Aren't those the best kind of surprises?' prompted Lady Fielding lightly. 'Lovely to speak to you again, Cassandra. We'll see you about half past twelve. 'Bye.'

'Goodbye.'

Cassandra put down the phone with some reluctance, and she was still standing staring at it when Mrs Temple appeared from the kitchen.

'I've finished doing those peas, Mrs Ravek,' she said, wiping her hands on her apron. 'And I've made a raspberry mousse for lunch. There are more than enough raspberries to make twelve pounds of jam.'

'Will there be enough for four?' enquired Cassandra flatly, expelling her breath rather heavily, and the housekeeper frowned.

'Bless you, you'll have enough jam——'

'Not jam, Mrs Temple. Mousse,' exclaimed Cassandra interrupting her. 'For lunch. Do we have plenty for four? I—Lady Fielding has just told me she and Sir Giles are in the area. They've invited themselves to lunch, and—and I don't know what Jay is going to say.'

'Oh, dear!' Mrs Temple sighed. 'That woman has the knack of creating awkward situations! Fancy her ringing this morning, when Mr Ravek's gone out! She couldn't have chosen a more convenient time.'

'Convenient?' Cassandra shook her head. 'What do you mean?'

'Well——' Mrs Temple clicked her tongue, 'knowing Mr Ravek, as I do, I doubt he'll welcome his mother here today. I mean, his having to go into Sutton Medlock for me this morning has upset his schedule, and now that his mother's coming . . .'

'Don't say any more,' muttered Cassandra, pushing

her hands into the pockets of the baggy dungarees she was wearing. 'I suppose he'll imagine I invited her. Oh, Mrs Temple, I can't even ring her back and cancel it. I don't know where she's staying.'

The sound of the Ferrari's engine interrupted their speculations, and presently Jay came striding through the open door of the porch carrying a cardboard box. He was wearing denims and a short-sleeved sweat shirt, and Cassandra's senses stirred as his dark gaze swept briefly over her.

'All present and correct,' he remarked, handing the box to Mrs Temple. 'What are you both looking so worried about? Don't tell me you've forgotten something.'

'No.' Cassandra caught her lower lip between her teeth and exchanged a look with the housekeeper. 'No, I—it's something else. Nothing to do with the jam-making.'

'What Mrs Ravek's trying to tell you is that your mother rang while you were out,' declared Mrs Temple, without preamble.

'My mother?' Jay's eyes narrowed. 'So?'

'So—she's coming to lunch,' muttered Cassandra unwillingly. 'She and—and your stepfather. They've been staying in the area, and they thought it was a good opportunity to—to meet me.'

Jay's expression was unreadable. 'You invited them?'

'I suppose so.' Cassandra found she could not let his mother take all the blame. 'Do you mind terribly?'

Jay took a deep breath. 'There's not much point now, is there?'

Mrs Temple slipped away, and Cassandra linked her hands together. 'You—you won't be able to write,' she murmured apologetically. 'I'm sorry.'

'I'll survive,' he retorted, shifting his weight from one foot to the other. 'I just wish you'd waited before making any arrangements.'

Cassandra felt a twinge of resentment. 'Are—are you ashamed of me, is that it?'

'Don't talk rubbish!'

'What is it, then?' Cassandra tilted her head defiantly. 'I'd like to meet your mother. That's not unnatural, is it?'

'Perhaps. In the circumstances.' Jay was abrupt.

'We are married, Jay.'

'Don't I know it?' His mouth tightened. 'Unfortunately, my mother doesn't know that you're pregnant!'

Cassandra groped weakly for the banister. 'She—doesn't know?'

'No.' Jay thrust his hands into his pockets. 'I saw no reason to tell her. It's nothing to do with her.'

'Jay, she's the baby's grandmother——'

'I know it.' Jay was indifferent.

'Then she has a right to know.'

'Why?' His eyes challenged hers. 'You've made no bones about the fact that once the baby's born you intend to get a divorce. I may be granted the courtesy of providing for my child, but I doubt I'll be given custody, don't you?'

Cassandra quivered. 'That's in the future——'

'Is it?' Jay's jaw hardened. 'I find it's very much in the present. It occupies my every waking minute. The only respite I get is when I write.'

'Then you must get a lot,' retorted Cassandra tersely. 'You seem to do nothing else but!'

'What would you have me do?' he demanded harshly. 'Spend my time with you? Torture myself by not touching you, watching you, *wanting* you! Oh, yes——' His lips twisted. 'That old dragon has raised its ugly head again. But don't worry, I haven't forgotten my promise. I'll keep out of your way, if you'll keep out of mine.' He walked across to the study door and thrust it open. 'Go and make yourself pretty for our visitors. I'll be in here, if you want me.'

If she wanted him!

In her bedroom, Cassandra acknowledged that she wanted him badly. Indeed, if his mother and stepfather's arrival had not been imminent she might well have told him so. As it was, she was faced with the prospect of entertaining his parents when all she really wanted to do was sort out her troubled feelings.

A full-length cream smock, with tiny flowers embroidered round the low neckline and scalloped hem, seemed the most attractive item in her limited wardrobe. It had no sleeves, which she thought was a disadvantage, but at least her arms were tanned and contrasted agreeably with the thin cotton. Her feet also were bare. She had not worn tights for weeks, and her legs had tanned accordingly and complemented her high-heeled sandals.

She heard the car arrive as she was descending the stairs, and Jay came out of the study to greet his parents as she reached the bottom step. His eyes appraised her burningly, lingering on the tell-tale peaks pressing against the material of her bodice, and then he slammed the study door abruptly, and strode out to the porch.

Cassandra didn't know what she had expected exactly, but Jay's mother was very definitely different from what she had imagined. To begin with, although she knew that Lady Fielding was over sixty, she was taken aback by her youthful appearance, and far from fitting the image of the sophisticated society matron, Jay's mother wore little make-up and dressed without fuss.

But as her mother-in-law got out of Sir Giles' Daimler, Cassandra immediately saw her resemblance to Jay. Like him, she was excessively dark, although her hair was now threaded with shades of grey, and her features mirrored his determination, even if they were softened by age and experience. Lady Fielding was wearing a casual linen slack suit, pale grey, with a cerise silk scarf knotted at her neck. Her hair was short and straight, like her son's, and her welcome to him was enthusiastic even if his was slightly less so.

'Don't tell me, I know—you didn't want us,' she declared, giving him a quick hug before turning to look at Cassandra. 'And now I can see why. Good heavens, the child's pregnant! And not too many weeks from her time, if I'm not mistaken.'

'Cass isn't a child, Mama. She's twenty-four,' retorted Jay flatly, turning to shake hands with his stepfather. 'Hello, Giles, good to see you. Come along in.'

'Thanks, James.' Giles Fielding was a tall spare man, in his early sixties, Cassandra estimated, and rather distinguished-looking. But he had a nice smile, which he bestowed on her as they were introduced, and he decried his wife's accusation by assuring Cassandra that her 'interesting' condition was extremely flattering. 'I'm sorry if we've swooped on you at an awkward time,' he added, allowing her to precede him indoors. 'But as soon as Alexa heard the news she couldn't wait to come and meet you.'

'The news?' Cassandra was aware that Jay was also listening to their conversation. 'What news?'

'Why, about the baby, of course,' Lady Fielding interjected, turning to look back at her. 'That girl we both know so well, James, Liz Lester, she told us. She said she thought we knew, but naturally I took that with a pinch of salt!'

'Liz?'

Cassandra's involuntary exclamation made Jay's mother arch her dark brows. 'Do you know her, too, Cass?' she asked in surprise. 'Well——' she looked at her son. 'I had no idea.'

Cassandra's brow creased. What did Lady Fielding mean? She had thought Liz's knowledge of Jay stemmed from the gossip columns syndicated throughout the country, that and the inside information she gleaned from the society parties she was invited to attend. She had only once suspected that Liz's contempt for her husband might have a more personal basis, but Liz herself had denied it so fiercely, she had dismissed the suggestion at once. Now, it seemed, she had been right to be suspicious of Liz. She had known Jay better than she had pretended. And what of Jay himself? What had their association meant to him? Enough that his mother had met her, thought Cassandra bitterly, feeling betrayed.

They all went into the drawing room to have a drink before lunch, and suddenly Jay was at her side, guiding her determinedly across the room to the tray. When Cassandra would have drawn back, his arm about her tightened perceptibly, and his lips against her ear whispered words she didn't want to hear.

'Stop looking as if I'd been unfaithful to you,' he muttered, his hand at her waist straying possessively over her ribcage. 'Liz and I once knew each other, that's all. I didn't go to bed with her, because it wasn't that kind of relationship.'

Cassandra found it difficult to speak, but she managed to choke scornfully: 'Do you expect me to believe that?'

'It's the truth.' Jay was laconic. 'I'll tell you about it, if you really want to know. But right now, let's keep up the pretence, shall we?'

'How?' she got out unsteadily, only to feel her heart thudding against her ribs as he bent his head towards hers. 'Like this,' he breathed, his mouth parting hers, driving all coherent thoughts out of her head.

'Well, really, James!' His mother's faintly accusing tones brought them apart, Cassandra moving quickly away, her face flushed with becoming colour. 'Must you make it so obvious you can't keep your hands off her? Good lord, you're embarrassing the child! Come and sit by me, Cassandra. I want to hear all about this romantic affair.'

'After lunch, Mama,' said Jay firmly, handing his mother a gin and tonic. 'The same for you, Giles? Or has living with Alexa driven you to something stronger?'

'Don't be insolent, darling.' Lady Fielding sipped her drink without evident offence. 'Giles is quite contented, aren't you, my sweet? Haven't you noticed how much weight he's put on since he retired from politics?'

The conversation continued in this vein until Mrs Temple announced that lunch was served. Lady Fielding had a few words with the housekeeper while she served the meal, and although Cassandra offered to help, Mrs Temple assured her she could cope.

The meal was delicious. Chilled melon was followed by a crisp salad, with a delightfully light quiche and new potatoes. The raspberry mousse was mouthwatering, and Jay's mother insisted she must be given the recipe before she left, and then they all adjourned to a shady spot in the garden. Mrs Temple had placed several comfortable loungers beneath the apple tree, and a small bamboo table supported the tray of coffee she had left for Cassandra to serve.

'Don't you usually rest in the afternoons?' Lady Fielding asked her daughter-in-law as Cassandra attended to the coffee cups. 'I mean, it's a long time ago, I know, but I always had to rest when I was carrying James.'

'Cass doesn't need advice from you, Mama,' Jay remarked impatiently, standing over the two women. 'Don't pour me any of that,' he added. 'Giles and I will get something stronger.'

'Yes, why don't you?' asked his mother, lying back in her chair and slanting a look up at him. 'You go and chat with Giles, James. Cassandra and I have a lot of time to make up.'

'Cass?'

With Jay's gaze on her, Cassandra was tempted to

give in to the almost overwhelming urge to ask him to stay with her. She didn't want a long, interrogative conversation with his mother. In truth, she wanted nothing so much as to be alone with her husband, but she knew that even if his parents were not here, that was an unlikely event.

'It's all right,' she murmured now, settling herself more comfortably on the lounger. 'I—yes, you go and have a drink with Sir Giles. Your mother and I will stay here.'

Nevertheless, after Jay and his stepfather had left them, Cassandra couldn't help wishing she had not been so accommodating. It was so hot, and in all honesty she would have welcomed the opportunity to lie down in her room for a while. She thought there was going to be a storm, and her clothes felt as if they were sticking to her.

'So—how long have you and James known one another?' enquired Lady Fielding with frank curiosity. 'I was so shocked when I learned he planned to get married. He had never mentioned a word about you to me.'

Cassandra folded her hands in her lap. 'It was—rather sudden,' she conceded. 'But——' she shrugged, unwilling to go into more personal details, 'you know how these things happen.'

'Yes.' Lady Fielding's eyes moved consideringly over her. 'You'll forgive me if I congratulate you, my dear. I would never have expected James to be trapped by that particular bait.'

Cassandra caught her breath. 'I beg your pardon——'

'Oh, now you're taking it the wrong way, my dear.' Jay's mother shook her head. 'I'm not criticising you. On the contrary, I've wanted James to get married for ages. I mean, he is my only offspring, and I can't wait to be a grandma. But, if I thought about it at all, I imagined he would marry someone—well, someone a little more sophisticated, shall we say? Someone who wouldn't gamble that getting herself pregnant would compel him to propose.'

Cassandra gasped. 'Lady Fielding, I did not——'

'My dear, don't get so upset! You don't have to defend yourself to me. I was like you once, only for me the gamble didn't pay off. But don't try to pretend that James didn't marry you because you were pregnant. I mean, I may not be much of a mathematician, but even I can add up to nine, and despite the fact that you got married in March, you won't carry that baby until Christmas!'

Cassandra's lips trembled. 'Just because I was pregnant when I got married it doesn't mean I expected your son to marry me,' she denied.

'Doesn't it?' Lady Fielding was infuriatingly sympathetic. 'Oh, Cassandra, don't look at me like that. I know what James is like. There've been dozens of girls angling for your position. Be thankful he decided to honour his responsibilities. In that way, I have to admit, he doesn't resemble his father.'

Cassandra glanced over her shoulder at the house. She wished Jay would come back. This was worse, so much worse than she had expected, and she was having the utmost difficulty in restraining herself from blurting exactly how she came to be Jay's wife.

But something, some ridiculous need to protect her husband, kept her silent, and Lady Fielding rambled on unchecked.

'I don't suppose James has told you about his father, has he?' she asked, and Cassandra had to concede that he had not. 'He was an American, you know. I met him in France just after the war.' She paused. 'I was in my middle twenties, and I suppose I was getting desperate.'

'Lady Fielding——'

'No, let me go on.' Jay's mother held up her hand. 'I

think you ought to know. You are James's wife, after all. You should know about the grandfather of the child you're carrying.' She sighed. 'Well, the simple explanation is that he was rich. He came from a wealthy Boston family. Unfortunately, he forgot to tell me he was also married.'

Cassandra bent her head. 'I'm sorry.'

'Yes, so was I.' Lady Fielding's lips twisted. 'I took a chance and I lost. It was only a small compensation to learn that the aircraft carrying him back to the United States had to ditch and there were no survivors.'

Cassandra sighed. 'I see.'

'It does have some relevance, you know.' Lady Fielding's dark brows drew together. 'James grew up hating his father for lying to me. I suppose he decided his child was not going to grow up hating him.'

Cassandra had been ready to make some trite response, but in spite of herself, she was stirred by what his mother said. Until then, she had not given much thought to the reasons behind Jay's determination. She had half believed he had exaggerated the scars he carried. But suddenly she had an insight into how he must have felt, growing up in a society that still abhorred the illegitimate child.

'I—I suppose it must have been hard for you,' she volunteered, and Lady Fielding spread her hands.

'It was. My parents were wonderful, of course, but they had little money and it was a struggle.'

'Did—did you ever think of—of not having the baby?' Cassandra had to know.

'Doesn't everyone?' Jay's mother gave a short laugh. 'Of course I thought about it. What girl in my position wouldn't? But believe it or not, I wanted my baby.' She grimaced. 'I suppose, deep down, I did care for James's father. At least I had a son to remember him by. He and his wife had only one daughter.'

It was a tragic story, but not unique for its time,

Cassandra guessed. There must have been dozens of
thwarted romances between people of different nationa-
lities, different cultures. And although she had not
wanted to hear his mother's story, now she was glad she
had; even if it did dispel for ever the faint hope that
there had been some other reason for his proposal.

Jay and his stepfather appeared just as Mrs Temple
was fetching out a tray of afternoon tea. 'Well? Have
you set the world to rights?' asked Lady Fielding,
awakening from the doze she had fallen into about half
an hour before. 'Hmm, tea! Just what I need, Mrs
Temple. And cakes, too. You have been busy!'

Jay's eyes went straight to his wife, and Cassandra
managed to meet his gaze composedly. 'Are you all
right? It isn't too hot out here for you?'

'No, I'm fine.' Cassandra got determinedly to her feet.
'But I'm going to stretch my legs now. Excuse me for a
few minutes, will you?'

Jay was waiting in the hall when she came back
downstairs, his hands pushed deep into his pockets. 'Are
you really okay?' he asked, his eyes narrowed and intent.
'What the hell was my mother saying to you? I could
hear her voice droning on and on.'

Cassandra sighed. 'She was telling me about your
father, actually,' she replied. 'Don't worry, she didn't
mention Liz. All she had to say in that connection was
that I'd been rather naïve using my pregnancy to make
you propose.'

'What!' Jay stared at her impatiently. 'Well, I suppose
you put her straight on that score.'

'I didn't, as it happens.' Cassandra hesitated. 'What
does it matter what she thinks? I doubt if she'd have
believed me anyway.'

Jay pulled his hands out of his pockets and reached
for her: 'Cass——'

'No.' She held herself away from him. 'Let me go. I
just thought it was none of her business, that's all. And

at least hearing about your father made me aware of what you must have suffered.'

'Cass!' Ignoring her pleas to release her, Jay pulled her close to him, the wedge of her stomach warm against his belly. 'Oh, Cass,' he bent his head and rested his forehead against her, 'I'm very much afraid I may not be able to give you that divorce, after all.'

'Why?' With the things she and his mother had discussed in the forefront of her mind, Cassandra could only think of one reason. 'Are you afraid your friends might suspect the truth if I divorce you?'

'No!' With a muffled oath, Jay propelled her away from him again. 'My God, doesn't any other reason occur to you?' He shook his head and strode abruptly towards the door. 'Forget it,' he muttered. 'I won't oppose you. You do what you like, so long as you don't try to stop me from seeing my son!'

CHAPTER TWELVE

IT was with an effort that Cassandra went outdoors again. She felt too confused, too distracted, to go on as if nothing had happened, and she was glad of Lady Fielding's inconsequent chatter to hide the gaps in the conversation. Jay avoided her eyes, conducting a desultory exchange with his stepfather, and not until his mother expressed a desire to look round the cottage did he exhibit any enthusiasm.

It was a natural consideration for her daughter-in-law's condition that made Lady Fielding defer to her son, and left alone with Sir Giles, Cassandra told herself she was glad of the breathing space. But she couldn't help wondering what Jay was saying to his mother, and wondering, too, why he had made that bewildering statement.

It was five o'clock when the skies opened and the storm that had been threatening all day released its fury. Within minutes, the paths around the cottage were running with water, and a spectacular streak of lightning accompanied by a resounding crack of thunder sent Lady Fielding hurrying to her husband's side.

'We can't possibly drive back to town in this, Giles,' she protested, gazing anxiously out the window. 'We'll have to find a hotel and book in for the night. We can ring Mrs Stewart and explain what's happened.'

Cassandra exchanged a look with Jay, and then took an unprecedented decision. 'You can stay here, if you like,' she declared, ignoring her husband's stunned reaction. 'We—er—we have a spare bedroom, don't we, Jay?

There's no earthly reason why your parents should go to a hotel.'

'I say, that's awfully good of you——' began Sir Giles, only to be overridden by his wife: 'We couldn't possibly impose,' she averred, after a thoughtful appraisal of her son's expression. 'It's very sweet of you, Cassandra, honestly, but we couldn't——'

'Stay!' Jay's harsh interjection halted her refusal. 'I— Cass is right. We do have three bedrooms, after all.' His dark eyes raked his wife's taut features. 'We wouldn't dream of turning you out, when we can share the same bed.'

Dinner was not an easy meal, although Cassandra did her best to avoid thinking of the pitfalls of what she had done. Nevertheless, with the storm showing little sign of abating outside, and the electricity showing every sign of failing inside, they were all a little tense.

Mrs Temple had done well to provide such a delicious meal at such short notice. And although it was just a simple collation of cold meats and salad with a home-made apple pie to follow, Lady Fielding and Sir Giles evidently found the food a welcome distraction.

Afterwards, Sir Giles proposed a game of bridge, but as Cassandra didn't play, Lady Fielding suggested whist instead. Although Cassandra wasn't keen, the cards at least gave her something to think about and she part-nered Jay's stepfather with assumed enthusiasm, apologising ruefully when they lost.

The lights finally gave out about ten-thirty, and Cassandra was relieved when Jay went out to the kitchen and came back with two lighted oil-lamps. 'They smoke a bit if you turn them up too high,' he said, explaining the principle to Sir Giles, and his mother declared with some asperity that he had become quite domesticated.

'Didn't you believe I could?' he countered, raising the lamp high so that he could see her face, and Lady Fielding shrugged.

'If what you tell me is true, I suppose I must accept it,' she responded, with a thoughtful look at her daughter-in-law. 'Well, I assume it's time for goodnights, Cassandra. Sleep well, darling. We'll see you both in the morning.'

After his parents had gone upstairs, Cassandra busied herself putting the cards away and clearing up the coffee cups and glasses they had used earlier. 'Leave them,' Jay exclaimed, apparently irritated by her industry, but she went on about her business, putting off the inevitable confrontation.

She and Jay were to sleep in the back bedroom, instead of the front. Mrs Temple had been up earlier and changed the sheets, and when Cassandra was sure their guests had settled down, she looked at last at her husband.

'Shall we go?' she suggested, knowing what she was inviting, but to her surprise Jay shook his head.

'You go,' he said. 'Take the lamp with you. You know how to turn it out, don't you? I can manage with a candle. I saw some in the cupboard in the kitchen.'

Cassandra stood her ground. 'You mean you're not coming to bed?'

'I mean I'm going to sleep on the couch,' explained Jay flatly. 'It was kind of you to offer my parents a bed, but I wouldn't dream of taking advantage of the situation. I told you before, it wouldn't happen again, and I meant it.'

Cassandra felt an awful fluttery feeling in the pit of her stomach, but she had to go on: 'You don't want to share my bed?'

Jay sighed. 'That question isn't worthy of an answer,' he declared. 'Go to bed, Cass. It's a warm night. It won't be the first time I've slept without a mattress.'

Still she lingered. 'I—I—and if I said I wanted you to come to bed?'

'*Cass!*'

'No, I mean it.' She licked her lips. 'I never intended for you to sleep down here, Jay. I—I'm willing to have you share my bed.'

'Cass!' He raked back his hair with fingers that she noticed were not quite steady. 'Cass, sharing your bed wouldn't be enough!'

'I know that.'

Jay half turned away from her so she was no longer in his line of vision. 'You don't know what you're saying. This afternoon——'

'This afternoon I was—hurt. I thought you were afraid of what your mother might have said about Liz——'

'Liz!' Jay almost spat the word. 'For God's sake, Cass, what could she have told you about Liz Lester? Unless you mean that her father and mine were one and the same!'

Cassandra moved round so that she could look into his face. 'Liz—Liz's father was—was the man——'

'—my mother had an affair with? Yes. Liz's mother married again after he died—an Englishman, Harold Lester. Liz was little more than a baby when her mother brought her to England.'

Cassandra shook her head. 'But does she know?'

'She does. My mother told her—Alexa's like that. I expect she saw it as a way of getting back at Liz's father through her.'

Cassandra tried to understand this. 'Then—you and Liz were—were what?'

'Didn't you know? That Liz used to work for the *Post*?' Jay sighed. 'Well, she did. I guess we both started there around the same time.'

Cassandra hesitated. 'But—did you——'

'Did I know who she was?' Jay grimaced. 'Of course. I made my mother tell me about my father at a very early age. I'm sure she told you that.'

'Well—perhaps.' Cassandra was beginning to see the pattern. She bit her lip before adding tentatively: 'I suppose Liz was attracted to you.'

Jay shrugged. 'Very briefly.'

Remembering Liz's bitterness, Cassandra thought it had been more than that, but she had to ask: 'And you?'

'Me!' Jay raised his eyes heavenward. 'Cass, she's my sister! My half-sister, anyway. I never thought of her like that.' He grimaced. 'Hell, she knows that!'

Cassandra lifted her shoulders. 'But why does she dislike you so?'

'Liz is not a very forgiving person. I guess she was badly hurt. Discovering her father had feet of clay meant a lot to her.' He paused. 'My mother can be pretty brutal, you know. I guess it's her Russian blood.'

Cassandra expelled her breath. 'I'm sorry.'

'For what?'

'Oh—for everything.' Cassandra ran embarrassed hands over her stomach. 'Mostly for believing Liz, I think.'

Jay picked up the oil lamp. 'I'm no saint,' he said flatly. 'I guess she had every justification for warning you about me. Look at you now!'

Cassandra looked down at her stomach and then up at him. 'I'm not sorry,' she said huskily, and she suddenly knew it was true. Even if this time with Jay was only a passing interlude, she knew now she would not have changed anything.

'Cass!' Jay stared at her unbelievingly for a moment and then with a groan of anguish he slipped his arm around her neck. 'Oh, Cass,' he breathed, pulling her close against him. 'If you only knew how I've wanted you to say that! Don't you know the only reason I married you was because I'm crazy about you? All that rubbish about my father and illegitimacy! Do you really think I'd have married a woman I didn't love? I wanted you. I still do. But how could I tell you I loved you, when all you wanted from me was a chance to show your independence?'

Cassandra turned her face against his neck. 'But—but you were so adamant——'

'Yes, well——' Jay's lips were against her hair. 'I do have some pride, you know, and it's taken quite a beating over this affair. Let's face it, you refused to see me again after that night in Cambridge, and I was feeling pretty sore by the time you showed up at my apartment.'

Cassandra quivered. 'You frightened me.'

'*I* frightened *you*?'

'Yes.' She paused. 'You made me lose my own identity. With—with Mike, it never happened. He—oh, our relationship was so different. I'd really begun to believe I couldn't feel love——'

'I know that.' Jay's fingers stroked her neck. 'But why did you fight me?' He frowned. 'Was it only because of Liz?'

Cassandra shook her head. 'I didn't want to get that involved with anyone ever again.' She sighed ruefully. 'I thought—oh, it sounds foolish now—I thought I'd be very sophisticated and have an affair. Then you were there, and it didn't seem like such a good idea after all.'

'Why not?'

He was insistent and she gave him a tremulous smile. 'I suppose because I knew I was falling in love with you, and I was afraid to give you that power over me. I wanted to be cool—detached; but with you it was impossible.'

'Lord, Cass——' He nuzzled her neck. 'And I thought you hated me for—well, for making you pregnant. You seemed to resent it so much. I began to despise myself.'

Cassandra sighed. 'I suppose, at first, I did resent it.' she admitted honestly. 'I was sure you'd only married me to ensure the baby had a father. Anything else— our—our attraction to one another—was purely physical. Something any other woman——'

Jay's unsteady breath fanned her forehead. 'Oh, Cass, if you only knew!' he muttered with feeling. 'Since we met there've been no other women. I can't summon any interest in anyone else. And I admit, I did try, at least before we were married.'

Cassandra's lips parted. 'I thought—those nights earlier in the year when you were going out——'

'Drinking,' he averred heavily. 'Dulling my senses so I didn't disgrace myself entirely by flinging myself on your mercy!'

'Oh, Jay!' She slid her arms around him, pressing herself closer. 'Let's go to bed.'

Cassandra awakened in the early hours of the following morning with the distinct awareness that all was not as it should be. At first she thought it was the unaccustomed warmth of Jay's body, curved close to her back beneath the thin sheet which covered them. But it was not. There was a discomforting constriction in the lower part of her abdomen, and as she lay there wondering if that was what had woken her, a distinctly unpleasant spasm of indigestion gripped her.

She blinked, wondering if the cream Mrs Temple had served with the apple pie at dinner had been entirely fresh, and then caught her breath as the indigestion swelled into something stronger.

The baby!

With a feeling of incredulity, she levered herself up on to her elbow, and the sudden movement caused Jay to stir and mumble in protest.

'It's the middle of the night,' he groaned, opening his eyes long enough to register that it was not yet light. 'Hmm, Cass, come back here. It's too early yet to get up.'

'You go back to sleep,' said Cassandra, levering herself to the edge of the bed. She wasn't totally cognisant of what happened in these matters, but she was sure that nothing was likely to happen for several hours yet. If indeed it was what she thought it was. The baby was not due for another three weeks, and the doctor had told her that first babies were often late. Nevertheless, she knew she would feel better if she was up and doing something, than lying here wondering what it could be.

'Cass!' Jay was fully awake now, and with a muffled oath he leaned over and tried the bedside lamp. It came on at once, and Cassandra breathed a sigh of relief. At least she would not have to start fiddling about with oil-lamps.

'I'm just going to get a drink,' she assured him, tying the cord of her silk dressing gown about her. 'You don't need to get up. I'll be perfectly all right.'

Jay sat up, cross-legged, the thin sheet outlining the muscled strength of his thighs. 'Cass,' he said, regarding her half impatiently, 'if you want a drink, let me get it. Come on, come back to bed.'

'No, I—I'm not tired,' she said, moving towards the door. 'Jay, please, don't worry about me. You're sleepy. Get some rest.'

His dark eyes moved possessively over her. Then, with unexpected perception, he said: 'It's the baby, isn't it? Something's wrong. For God's sake, Cass, don't keep it from me!'

'Nothing's wrong.' Her lips parted in faint amusement. 'Jay, it might be that the baby's coming—sooner than we expected.'

'God!' With a lithe movement Jay sprang out of bed, dragging on his own navy dressing gown to cover his nakedness. 'I'll call the doctor,' he said, regarding her with unfeigned concern. 'I'd better take you to the hospital myself. Heaven knows how long an ambulance might take to get here after all the rain.'

'Jay!' Cassandra put a reassuring hand on his sleeve. 'Darling, it may have slipped your notice, but the storm's over. It's not raining any more.' She grimaced. 'And stop panicking. Nothing's going to happen for hours!'

'So you say.' He raked back his hair with unsteady fingers. 'God, I feel so helpless! I knew I should have slept downstairs.'

Cassandra gurgled with laughter. 'Oh, Jay, don't be so silly. Besides,' she cast him an artful look, 'I don't remember you offered much protest last night.'

Jay's eyes darkened. 'Don't tease me. Tell me how you really feel. Oh, Cass,' he took her into his arms, 'I don't know what I'd do if anything happened to you now.'

'Nothing's going to happen to me,' she assured him, feeling amazingly confident all of a sudden. 'Come on, I'll make you some tea.'

'I'll make *you* some tea,' asserted Jay flatly. 'I need something stronger.'

Cassandra's baby was born at lunchtime. After a remarkably brief labour, an eight-pound baby boy made his entry into the world just after twelve o'clock, and Jay was there to see his son delivered. Cassandra was exhausted but exhilarated by the experience, and when Jay squatted down beside her to tell her the good news, she summoned up a special smile just for him.

'You wait until you see him,' he said, glancing back to where a nurse was wrapping the tiny body in a warm wrapper. 'He's beautiful. Just like his mother. Although I have to admit,' he grimaced, 'he doesn't have your complexion.'

Cassandra let him carry her hand to his lips. 'Our son,' she breathed, meeting his dark eyes. 'What are we going to call him?'

David Alexei Ravek was christened a month later, at the little church in Combe Bassett. Jay's parents were there, and Thea, and Mike's mother made a special effort to speak to her daughter-in-law alone.

'Are you happy?' she asked, gazing anxiously into Cassandra's green eyes. 'I must know. You don't regret—well, my part in this affair? I know that if I hadn't been so adamant, you would never have gone to see Jay.'

'Thank God you were,' exclaimed Cassandra fervently, giving her a hug. 'Oh, darling, I don't want to hurt you, but I've never been so happy!' She paused. 'I didn't know it could be like this, you see.' She shook her head. 'You were very perceptive. You realised how I felt long before I did.'

'I'm so glad.' Thea smiled at her. 'And it doesn't hurt me, darling. She shrugged. 'Mike is dead. It's your happiness that's important to me now.'

'Thank you, Thea.'

'Don't thank me, Cass. Thank Jay. He's responsible for this wonderful change in your life.' She chuckled. 'Perhaps I can take one small piece of credit, though. I knew how he felt about you right from the beginning.'

'You did?' Cassandra arched her brows. 'Go on.'

'Well——' Thea was reluctant now, 'you remember that weekend you went up to Cambridge?'

'Will I ever forget?'

'And how Jay came after you?' Thea hesitated. 'I had plenty of time afterwards to regret what I'd done by giving him the name of your hotel, but I have to tell you, I didn't do it without cause.'

'No?'

'No.' Thea was firm. 'Jay came to my apartment, as you know. I don't think he'd slept all night.' She frowned. 'At first, I said I didn't know where you were. It was what I thought you would have wanted me to say. But then—well, he told me how he felt about you, that he cared about you and that he believed you cared about him, too, only you were too scared to admit it.'

'Jay said that?' Cassandra caught her breath. 'But you never said!'

'How could I? You came back swearing it had all been a mistake, that you didn't intend seeing him again. How could I tell you when he so obviously hadn't?'

Cassandra shook her head. 'I thought—oh, you know what I thought. Liz said there had been so many other girls . . .'

'Well, we know now that Liz had her own reasons for being bitchy, don't we?' remarked Thea drily. 'Cass, Liz was jealous of you, can't you see? She resented Jay just as much for the fact that he was her half-brother as for his being her father's son. Does that make sense to you? I think once she fancied herself in love with him. When it didn't work out, she blamed him.'

Cassandra nodded. 'Poor Liz!'

'Poor Liz nothing. She did her best to ruin your life,' declared Thea flatly. 'Thank goodness you came to your senses. I knew Jay was the man to make you happy.'

Jay's arm came across his wife's shoulders. 'Fortune-telling, Thea?' he asked teasingly, his hand at Cassandra's nape. 'Perhaps you can tell me whether my book's going to be any good. I'd be interested to have your opinion.'

'If what Cass tells me is true, it's going to be a best-seller,' said Thea, including them both in her smile. 'Though I hear from Chris that you've got other investments now. Is it true, Cass? Is Jay the new partner in the business?'

'A sleeping partner,' put in Jay ruefully, and Cassandra playfully pushed her fist into his ribs.

'He didn't tell me, you know,' she declared. 'If Chris hadn't spilled the beans, I'd never have known that Jay had provided the cash backing we so desperately needed.'

'It was the least I could do,' averred Jay humorously. 'In the circumstances.'

Cassandra's warm colour was appealing, and Thea gave a resigned shake of her head. 'I suppose when you move to this house in Buckinghamshire, you'll never be out of the office, Cass.'

'Oh, no.' Cassandra was very definite about that. 'Penny, she's the girl Chris and Paul took on when I left, is a permanent fixture now. And we're only moving to Buckinghamshire because Jay has found a house big enough to provide a nursery and guestroom, as well as his study. There's even a studio for me, over the garage, but although Chris says I can freelance, I don't think I'll be spending too much time there during the next few months.'

'Well, not during the next few weeks anyway,' agreed Thea firmly. 'Now, remember, I'll be back on Thursday, so don't worry about a thing. David Alexei will be perfectly safe with me.'

'I'm sure he will.' Cassandra glanced across the room to where Jay's mother was proudly displaying her six-week-old grandson to Guy and Helen Conway.

'I've got the reservations,' said Jay, with some satisfaction. 'The plane leaves at twelve o'clock Friday, and we should be in our hotel by early evening local time.'

'Bermuda,' sighed Cassandra dreamily. 'I can hardly believe it.'

'You will,' murmured Jay, bestowing an intimate kiss on her parted lips, and Thea turned away, content that she was no longer needed.

FREE-an exclusive Anne Mather title, MELTING FIRE

At Mills & Boon we value very highly the opinion of our readers. What <u>you</u> tell us about what you like in romantic reading is important to us.

So if you will tell us which Mills & Boon romance you have most enjoyed reading lately, we will send you a copy of MELTING FIRE by Anne Mather – absolutely FREE.

There are no snags, no hidden charges. It's absolutely FREE.

Just send us your answer to our question, and help us to bring you the best in romantic reading.

CLAIM YOUR FREE BOOK NOW

Simply fill in details below, cut out and post to: Mills & Boon Reader Service, FREEPOST, P.O. Box 236, Croydon, Surrey CR9 9EL.

— — — — — — — — — — — — — — — — —

The Mills & Boon story I have most enjoyed during the past 6 months is:

TITLE _____

AUTHOR_____ BLOCK LETTERS, PLEASE

NAME (Mrs/Miss) _____ EP4

ADDRESS _____

_____

_____ POST CODE _____

Offer restricted to ONE Free Book a year per household. Applies only in U.K. and Eire. CUT OUT AND POST TODAY – NO STAMP NEEDED.

Mills & Boon
the rose of romance